JOSÉ RAMÓN TORRES

Acknowledgments

I would like to thank Louise Durkin, Robin Myers, Jackie Cannon, Maggie Carr and Elizabeth Torres for helping me complete this English version of the Spanish original. Without their time, patience, valuable advice and useful interventions, I would still be struggling with words.

To my wife Liz and my children Daniel and Amelia,

for the time this book has taken away from them.

Contents

The Press Release

In view of the tragic death of a guard at the Peruvian Embassy and given the tolerant attitude adopted toward such criminals by the Peruvian government, the government of the Republic of Cuba has decided to withdraw protection from said diplomatic mission. The diplomatic staff will, henceforth, be fully responsible for what happens in the embassy. We cannot protect embassies that do not cooperate with their own protection.
(*Granma* daily newspaper, Havana, Cuba, Friday 4 April, 1980)

The Gardens

As the sun sets on Saturday, April 5, the number of asylum seekers approaches ten thousand. Swarms of people are battling their way to the embassy in pursuit of exile. Among those who have managed to make it inside are a group of students from Havana University who arrived at around nine in the morning, three bus drivers who abandoned their vehicles mid-route, and a tanker driver who came to deliver water and decided to end his rounds right then and there.

Three young men have just arrived, half naked, straight from the beach. Before heading in, one of them flags down a taxi, scribbles his family's address on a scrap of paper, and asks the driver to bring them to the embassy. He also gives him a watch, a baseball cap, a snorkeling mask, and the promise that this will be the best fare of his life.

"Remember the woman who said she'd given birth here and asked to be urgently flown out to Peru?" a white-haired woman asks another leaning against the dog kennel. "Well, turns out she made off with the baby in a sheet all covered in blood from the maternity hospital on Línea."

"No!"

"Oh, yes, my dear, there's not a word that isn't true."

A few yards from the two women, a man wrapped in a Peruvian flag is shouting into the crowd.

"No one can shoot at me. Not the police, not the army. No one! I am Peru itself. No one can touch me."

In the grounds of the mansion, Ángel looks on in awe and pity at the spectacle he is a part of. He's not at all convinced by what the nutcase with the flag is saying, but he has more pressing things to worry about — such as the dangerous proximity of a man eyeing him fixedly from the ground, with a nose that looks as if it's been flattened in a fistfight. The guy, he notices, is carrying a long, sharp-toothed saw with a bandaged handle. Is he really looking at Ángel, or is Ángel imagining the evil gaze? Could it be fear playing tricks on the mind, fabricating threats that don't really exist?

Fear, sweat and hunger. Perhaps these are the primary elements, the building blocks of life. What else is there between the tip of Maisí and Cape San Antonio? In Guantánamo, Holguín, Camagüey, Cienfuegos, Matanzas, or Pinar del Río? Is there anywhere, any corner of this island, where hunger, sweat and fear don't rule our lives and invade our dreams?

*****

With every passing minute, people arrive in their hundreds. The mood is electric. On Saturday, a young couple who wanted to go home were given a serious beating by a bunch of thugs. No knives were used on that occasion but, yesterday, a poor wretch who had climbed a mango tree found himself faced with an angry mob threatening to slit his throat — and all because a bit of dirt had fallen from his shoes. This was not how Ángel had pictured asylum. He had imagined a haven of peace and unity, not a preview of hell itself. Even going for a drink of water or taking a pee was becoming dangerous. God knows what might happen if you were to accidentally bump someone's elbow or step on their toes. The survival strategy is to form groups and guard the spot of anyone absent for a few minutes, but even this has led to clashes. What if his foot inadvertently brushes against the leg of the pug-nosed guy and he ends up with a gaping wound on his heel that won't stop bleeding? He'd have to leave the embassy, dragging his injured foot behind him.

Three days ago, Ángel could never have pictured himself in a situation like this, not even in his wildest dreams. But perhaps we never really decide anything. Circumstances. Everything is always ultimately governed by circumstances, he thinks. And Mireya, who has dragged him here. Is Mireya a circumstance? What a stupid thing to think, he quickly tells himself. At any other time, he would have laughed, but this is no time for laughing. He's sweating and hungry. And frightened — why deny it? He's very frightened. He's gotten to know the place quite well, having been here three days now, roughing it, without a shower and barely a bite to eat, and he's seen a stretch of fence he could jump to get out. But the crowd responds violently to the slightest hint of desertion.

Ángel gets on his toes and stretches his neck, but he still can't see much further through the crowd. He thinks he should muster the courage to check out whether the latest uproar has anything to do with the few measly boxes of food supplied by the government, but tells himself that, at barely forty, it's not worth risking his skinny neck for such a meager reward. In any case, it's always the thugs who end up with the food. They sweat just like everyone else but are not as frightened and don't go as hungry.

*****

3

Mireya's daughter, who just turned twelve, isn't saying much — but she's not looking too good either, her eyes underscored by dark purple shadows, her gaze sad and dismayed. Ángel strokes her hair. It's strange, he thinks, that he should be worrying about Sofía when he's about to leave his own kids behind, maybe forever. If he weren't so tired, so overwhelmed by the goddamned circumstances, he might shed a tear for them, but he knows that his internal lament has been stifled, choked up for far too long; it won't come to the surface now.

He wonders whether Eduardo has been given a pass. If he goes to the tenement room, he'll find the farewell note Ángel left on the table for him. And what about Emilia? Ángel is confident that his daughter and Pepe will get by on their own, as they've done so far. He's not as worried about them as he is about little Eduardo, his Eduardito. When the boy is faced with the fact that his father has gone into exile behind his back, he'll never forgive him.

A gentle breeze carries a smell of vegetation that takes Ángel back to his childhood, to the exhilaration he would feel when he helped clean and prepare a pig just killed by his father. He remembers shaving it with a razor and piping hot water, carefully placing a branch from the guava tree in the slit of its throat and turning it on the spit.

While Ángel reminisces, a female voice begins to sing the Cuban national anthem and the song spreads listlessly among the asylum seekers, as if their weary bodies were resonating, the sound waves reverberating in their bones. Eyes meet and console each other. Expressionless. Impassive.

*****

It's now approaching six o'clock in the evening and, from his place in the line to use the water tap, Ángel sees two Alfa Romeos arriving at the corner of 72nd Street and Fifth

Avenue, alongside a sleek black car. Word quickly spreads that it's Fidel's famous ZIL. At various times in his life, Ángel has entertained the notion that the Commander-in-Chief is a deity clothed in olive green, but he is now able to see, as plain as day, that The Man exists in the flesh. It is the first time Ángel has been so close to him and he wonders what made him decide to come to the embassy in person. One thing's for sure: the asylum seekers' fate will be sealed by what the Comandante says and does in the coming hours.

The synapses collide in Ángel's brain. What might have brought Fidel to the embassy? Amid mounting tensions with Venezuela and Peru over the right to seek refuge in their diplomatic missions in Havana, The Boss must have met with the high command to discuss the possibility of withdrawing police protection from both embassies.

"My advisors think there'll be trouble if we withdraw the guards," someone like the Minister of the Interior or the Head of State Security may have warned.

"We have to step carefully in a situation like this. Removing protection from any embassy, not just the Peruvian one, has its risks," Fidel's brother, army general and Minister of the Armed Forces, may have cautioned.

This morning, however, perhaps on seeing a report strewn across his desk in the Palacio de la Revolución estimating the number of asylum seekers at ten thousand, the Comandante probably decided he should go and see for himself.

On the way to the embassy, he must have felt the grip of the tires on the road as the ZIL crossed Miramar's even-numbered streets. Ángel imagines this part of the journey impregnated with the smell of the sea but perhaps The Man was too distracted to notice it. Maybe he delighted in the fact that the neighborhood's grand buildings, the former hotels and casinos, no longer serve their original purpose? He has rid the place of its white-collar thieves and now the streets are filled with uniformed schoolchildren with books and smiling faces, friends of Cuba from foreign shores, and workers committed to the socialist cause. The palatial homes abandoned by the wealthy Cubans who had fled the island with the triumph of the Revolution were initially turned into schools or dormitories for students from outside Havana, and then, as educational centers were progressively built across the country, into embassies or the offices of foreign companies doing business in Cuba. There is no trace of the seedy gambling dens and brothels that, prior to 1959, unashamedly lined the south side of the avenue. They were no more than a stone's throw away from the exclusive nautical and social clubs on the north side, after the roundabout next to what used to be the Coney Island amusement park.

As Ángel silently recites this party line patter, conscious of it replaying in his mind like a catchy tune, like the nursery rhymes his mother used to sing to him when he was a child, the Comandante rolls down the back window of the ZIL, which has now come to a halt. He can see the people on the roof of the building, their arms raised, forming the victory sign in defiance at the helicopter hovering overhead. The Man must be wondering whether he's gone too far. All he probably wanted to do was teach Peru and Venezuela a lesson for backing repeated attempts by islanders to seek asylum. But now this mess threatens to overshadow his efforts at détente. The island has not only been enjoying a honeymoon period with its powerful enemy, but even moments of outright glory on the international scene. It's successfully taking on one of the world's strongest armies in Angola. It has hosted events such as the 11th World Festival of Youth and Students in 1978, or the Summit of the Non-Aligned Movement in 1979.

The Comandante gets out of the car, closes the door with purpose and takes a few strides toward the embassy gates. The hundreds of asylum seekers pressed against the fence move back in silence. An official makes his way through the crowd and out onto the street. Ángel wonders if it's just any old staff member or the business or cultural attaché, as the ambassador wouldn't be there at such an unearthly hour. In any case, Fidel says a few words to the Peruvian, puts an arm around his shoulder, and leads him to the ZIL.

*****

An eerie silence has reigned for most of the morning. Until a sentence — a short series of simple sounds arranged to obey an arbitrary order and meaning — breathes new life into the eleven thousand bodies packed together on the lawn, the roof, the dog kennel, and in the trees.

"They're giving safe-conducts!"

The rumors are confirmed in under ten minutes: the government is giving out permits that allow the asylum seekers to go home and come back whenever they like; all they have to do is ask for one. The embassy will take care of the formalities and they'll be allowed to leave as soon as the host country approves their application. It can't be another "report" from "The Telephone Man" — the guy who managed to get hold of a phone from inside the embassy and connect it as an extension in the garden — as the Peruvians retrieved the device a couple of days ago. It was thanks to him that news of any negotiations between the Peruvian and Cuban authorities had been leaked to the crowd, which then broadcast it, commented on it and distorted it at will, within seconds.

A number of asylum seekers have already been interviewed by embassy officials and are going home. The interview, they say, consists of an informal chat during which one of the Peruvians tries to talk them out of seeking political asylum and then, on seeing that they insist, gives them a letter of safe conduct. The meeting is then politely brought to a close without further ado.

Some are starting to leave and have no intention of coming back unless it is strictly necessary. Many others are refusing to go.

"Ángel, this girl is going to pass out on us," Mireya snaps. The frown remains etched on her face. "Go and check things out, for God's sake, and see if you can get something to eat."

"But I've just walked around and didn't find anything. I'll bring a wet handkerchief to cool her down. If they've started giving out letters of safe conduct, it means things are beginning to move."

"The problem with you is you don't have the balls to face those guys and tell them there are kids here who haven't eaten for days."

"It's not that, Mireya. They only throw a few cartons of food over the fence. And I bet you anything they only do it to watch us killing each other over them. Have you seen one? Do you know what's in them? You know you can go to the medical checkpoint to have your blood pressure taken and get a glass of water with sugar. Why don't you go and see if you can bring it for Sofía? You have to try and understand..."

"You're the one who doesn't understand anything. You've always got your head in the clouds. I don't know why the hell I brought you with me. All you do is get in the way."

Ángel says nothing. What can he say? He has only himself to blame for blindly going along with her. He wonders what possessed him to get caught up in such a mess.

Back on Friday afternoon, he had reached Mireya's place covered in sweat, exhausted after a hard day's slog at the workshop and a long walk in the blazing sun. Closing the door, he stopped for a few seconds to take a deep breath and feel the cool of the marble stairs and the tiled walls, leaving behind the dust, heat and noise of the street. Already feeling some sense of relief, he slowly started to climb the stairs, announcing his arrival as he went. When no one replied, he decided to pause again and enjoy the peace and quiet. It felt good to have a moment alone.

"You're early, hon! I'm so glad! You must have read my mind!"

Ángel responded with a heavy sigh. He could just make out Mireya's outline at the top of the stairs, the natural light of the inner patio shining behind her.

"Did you hear wha' happened? They've withdrawn protection from the Peruvian Embassy 'cause a group of guys crashed the gates with a bus 'n' killed one of the guards."

It was unusual for Mireya to come out onto the landing to welcome him, and puzzling to hear her struggling to get the words out quickly enough as she started down the stairs toward him.

"Alfredo brought the newspaper. I had to beg him to let me hang on to it. Here, read it for yourself."

"Give me a minute, will you? Give me a chance to get in first," protested Ángel as he made his way up the stairs.

"He told me he couldn't wait, honey, but, if we go with him, he says we can stay at his family's house in Hialeah when we get to the States."

"Hang on a second. Have you both lost your minds? What is Alfredo going to do in the States with only one eye and no English? And that's just for starters."

Agitated, Mireya turned and marched back up the half-flight of stairs. On reaching the landing, she drew a deep breath and retorted, "His brother is head of maintenance at a hotel and part-owner of a garage in Miami Beach, did you know that? He can help you get a job as soon as you get there — for starters. So don't be so flippant."

"Hotel? Garage? What the…?"

"I'll tell you what it is. Just listen to me for a minute, will you? Tons of people have already gotten in and there are truckloads more coming from the provinces. Once you're inside, it's Peruvian territory and the government can't do anything. We need to move fast though. You know how these things go."

Ángel went to sit down in one of the two wicker armchairs close to the balcony, holding the *Granma* she had thrust into his hands. He started to read the government communiqué and, unable to explain why, began counting the times the words "government" and "embassy" appeared, going over them with the tip of his index finger.

"Have you read it or not? What are you doing?" Mireya asked, disconcerted.

"Trying to count some words," he muttered.

"What? Is that all you can do at a time like this, Ángel Ribot?"

Rather than attempting a response, he put the newspaper down on his knees, rested his elbows on the arms of the chair, lowered his head until his face lay buried in his hands, and tried to gather his thoughts. With a decision like this, Mireya and her daughter were risking their future — and his too, for that matter.

He took a cigar from his shirt pocket. He'd been looking forward to the idea of sitting back and enjoying it, but any hopes of a relaxing evening were gone, no matter how good the cigar. Using his front teeth, he made a small opening just above the line where the cap met the wrapper, then gently pressed the cigar, rolling it between his thumb and index finger. It wasn't a select Habano, but it was well finished, had a good sheen, uniform color, and smelled of fresh tobacco. On top of that, it had been given to him, and you don't look a gift horse in the mouth.

Noticing Mireya coming over to him again, he spoke to her in a calm, steady voice.

"Why don't you sit down and relax for a minute, Mireya? This isn't as simple as it seems. We're both nearing forty and don't speak a word of English. If by any chance we can't get from Peru to the States, we'll be even worse off than we are here. That's if we manage to get out of the country at all. If we don't, we're going to be in real trouble."

"But, Ángel, don't you realize that entering the embassy now that they've removed the guards is not what they call an 'act of force'? They're not going to take reprisals, quite simply because they can't. There are already hundreds of people in there and thousands more are on their way. Ángel, we can't afford to mess around. Eduardo, poor soul, is stuck in the military and Emilia is off at the beach in Boca Ciega or Guanabo."

Poor soul, he thought. Poor souls, all of us; lost souls in a living hell. But he kept his thoughts to himself and simply asked, "Didn't Emilia leave you an address or a phone number?"

"Oh, Angelito! You know your daughter, don't you?"

"Dammit! Just when we need to be together!"

"You're telling me." Mireya paused, went to him, and stroked the back of his hand. "Listen, hun. Emilia has a life of her own now and a future with Pepe. He's been a political prisoner. Their exit papers could come through anytime."

"I know," he says, shaking his head helplessly. "It's just…"

"Shh. I'm telling it like it is because you'll regret it later. You've never had a chance to leave the country before. You don't have anyone abroad, no one to get you out. Neither you nor Eduardo. Not even anyone who'd invite you to go just for a few months. You can apply to have Eduardo join you once you're in the States or, at worst, in Peru. You just make up your mind while I get some jewelry and documents together."

Seeing the minutes pass and with no sight or sound of Ángel, Mireya stormed back into the living room. There he was, right where she had left him, stock-still in the armchair, the folded newspaper in one hand and the lit cigar in the other.

"Look, Ángel," she snapped, "I didn't go without you because I'm not the kind of person who does that shit. I knew it wouldn't be long before you got here, so I didn't want to go and get you from work and raise suspicion. I was planning on stopping by your room if I saw you were running later than usual. But you're here now, that's what matters, and there's no more time to waste. You can stay here, relax and smoke your cigar if you like. My conscience is totally clean. This is the chance we've been waiting for, the opportunity we've been talking about for so long; and I don't intend to waste it. I swear this on the life of that daughter of mine, who matters more to me than anything else in the world."

That daughter of hers has now gone for almost a week with barely any food or sleep and looks like death. It breaks Ángel's heart just to look at her. She's nothing but skin and bone, poor thing. He remembers her at the dining table Friday afternoon, sharpening a pencil and tracing a map. But her mother's short temper is too hard to cope with and it makes no sense for him to stay with her for the rest of his days. There was a time, after so many uphill battles had left him sapped of strength and hope, when he found just what he needed in Mireya. It was she who had saved him from bitterness, solitude and self-destruction. But things had changed over time, and not for the better. Now, to top it all off, she wants him to abandon Emilia and Eduardo.

"You're the one who doesn't understand anything. You've always got your head in the clouds. I don't know why the hell I brought you with me. All you do is get in the way." Her scornful words continue to reverberate in his ears. To shake them off, he rallies his lungs, vocal cords, tongue and facial muscles. Only then does his voice come to him, as if belonging to someone else.

"Things are not always the way you want them to be, Mireya. I don't even know why I'm wasting my breath trying to get through to you. Anything I tell you goes in one ear and out the other. Listen, since you say the only thing I do is get in the way, let me tell you that I only came to protect the two of you. You have no idea what kind of mess you're getting yourself into — and dragging Sofía along with you. Just look around you."

"What...?"

"Let me finish. You can go to Peru, to the States, to wherever the hell you want. But count me out."

It feels, indeed, as if he's not the one stringing together the sentences but an inner demon on a rampage he can't control.

"I'm going back home the same way I came, with no letter of safe conduct, no passport, no nothing. And I'd better shut up now because my blood pressure is going through the roof."

His last words, uttered with labored breath, fade out as he turns his back to the woman.

"Don't you dare," she shouts, after mumbling an insult too faint for Ángel to hear. "We haven't spent a whole week here just to split up now. We have to hang in till the end if we want a better life."

But Ángel is no longer listening. He has started to make his way through the crowd. He doesn't want to hear this group's radio or the other group's gossip. He shoves, pushes, and manages to head toward the escape route he's already spotted. As he goes, he reflects that his ideas have been clashing with those of his fellow asylum seekers for a while. Of course, they're bound to clash. There's nothing heroic, brave or patriotic about the absurd demonstrations of force he's witnessed over the last few days. The

Revolution is right to constantly remind the public about the real acts of bravery demonstrated by the Cuban people.

"You can all go to hell!" he exclaims under his breath, just after bumping into the pug-nosed guy who had whiled away the time staring at him.

If I have to die here with a knife in my gut, so be it, he ponders a few yards from the fence. His heart is pounding and regret slithers through his innards like a snake. The blood throbs in his temples and beads of sweat roll down his face, stinging his eyes. Suddenly, with a spryness he could never have imagined, he jumps over the fence and onto the street.

"There goes another infiltrator!"

He starts to run, not looking back.

"Traitor!"

"Son of a bitch!"

Stones roll by on either side of him. One of the bigger ones comes to rest beside the remains of a Young Communists Union card lying next to a drain.

Down with the Worms

Isabel punches down on the blade of the knife laid flat over two cloves of garlic after slicing off the ends. She removes their skin, chops them into fine pieces and adds them to the diced onion already frying in lard. Before starting on the green pepper, she glances toward the half-plastered living room, where her brother-in-law is taking a telegram from his shirt pocket and laying it on the table in front of Felo.

"They've given me seventy-two hours to get to the gas company and pay up, otherwise they're going to cut me off," she hears Ángel say.

She checks to see whether the rice is done and the chickpeas soft, adds the fried onion and garlic into the pressure cooker, and leaves the stew to simmer with the lid off. Then she takes a cloth and wipes down the white enamel of the Boss range cooker, still almost as good as new after thirty years. The two kerosene burners give off a dirty but powerful flame thanks to her brother-in-law, who adjusts them regularly.

"It's all work, work, work. And they never lose. They never make a mistake in your favor. They'd rob their own mothers. Who the hell do they think they are?" Ángel shouts, waving the piece of paper in front of his brother's face.

"Oh, no. He's started talking shit again," Felo protests, looking up at the ceiling.

"I'm not talking shit. Hear me out, will you? How much do I earn a month as an A-grade mechanic? Two hundred and forty pesos. OK? Keep that number in your head and now start from zero and add these up. A pack and a half of cigs a day, seventy-two pesos. Plus the thirty pesos I give Eduardito, that's a hundred and two."

Ángel's words are slowing — not because he's calming down but because he's drunk, assumes Isabel, who can smell the reek of alcohol from the kitchen.

"At least fifteen pesos for food rations," he carries on. "That's a hundred and seventeen, plus about thirty to buy extra oil, rice, sugar and coffee, and we're already up to a hundred and forty-seven. Are you following me? Now add the fifty cents a day spent on lunch, plus coffee, snacks and the bus fare to work. Let's say fifty pesos a month. That's already two hundred. Then ten for electricity and the sixteen I'm paying toward the fridge. Two hundred and twenty-six. Add the gas bill and what's left? Next to nothing! And I haven't even been out to a restaurant, bought myself a shirt or had a shot of rum."

Isabel looks on, secretly admiring Ángel's features, more regular and chiseled than her husband's. She thinks back to when Ángel stopped by a couple of days ago, drunk yet again, boasting about the money he was making on the side, on top of his official wage. He'd better not ask Felo to lend him any because he's not going to like it. It's not Felo's fault his brother is already broke a week after payday. She also watches her husband's tired gestures of resignation, until the irritation welling up inside him erupts.

"Restaurant? What the hell are you talking about?"

"Let me finish."

"What you need to do is lay off the bottle and stop talking so much bullshit. Alcohol doesn't care what you do for a living, whether you're a mechanic or a brain surgeon or a shoeshiner, whether you're a nice guy or an idiot, whether you're black, white or Chinese. When it gets hold of you, it gets you by the balls and won't let go until it kills you. Are you listening to me?"

There should be enough with rice, beans and a fried egg, Isabel reckons as she serves three portions of rice, puts a couple of tablespoons of lard in the hot frying pan, and spreads it evenly over the surface with a circular movement. She serves the steaming hot chickpeas in three deep plates. Some saltines would have been nice, she thinks, but there are none left. Without wasting a second, she breaks one, two, three eggs into the frying pan. As soon as they start frying, she cuts the whites with the edge of the aluminum skimmer and, in no time at all, places an egg sprinkled with salt on each plate of white rice.

"Hey, I like a drink but I'm no wino!" Ángel protests.

"Can you stop drinking? Can you? Be honest with yourself. You've been hitting the bottle for so long now you're hooked, and you've got nobody to blame but yourself. You can't function without a drink and you have to start by accepting it if you want to kick the habit. Of course, since all your friends are a bunch of drunks…"

"Let me get a word in, will you?"

"And I don't want you coming to this house and criticizing the Revolution when it's given you…"

"For fuck's sake, now you can't even…"

"Clear the table — I'm going to put the food out now," Isabel interrupts, peeking her head into the living room.

"No one's getting any food here today! I've had enough of this damn shit!" shouts Felo, his face deformed with rage. "Let's see who else will put up with your drunken rants. How many times do we have to tell you we don't want you drunk in this house?"

Ángel gets up and walks over to the kitchen stove to light his cigarette, after trying in vain with the last match in his box, which now lies empty on the table.

"Drunk? Drunk? Give me a fucking break, will you?" he remonstrates as he walks back into the living room, smoking.

Isabel winces as Felo thumps the table and jumps to his feet.

"There's no damn food for you here today, you hear me? The party's over. We're not running a hotel here. You can go to hell and eat, for all I care. And you won't be getting any more money out of me. Not a cent, dammit! Not even if you're dying, I swear on our mother's grave, may she rest in peace."

"It's over," Ángel stammers, his eyelids drooping.

"But don't you realize you're killing yourself, you piece of shit?" Felo turns his back without waiting for a response. With a gesture of despair, he walks away, grumbling to himself. "Why the hell do I waste my breath on him when he never listens to a word I say?"

"It's over. Right. It's over," repeats Ángel as he walks out the door.

*****

Minutes later, Ángel is staggering down Infanta Street, carrying the canvas bag his sister-in-law had hastily managed to give him, filled with a pound of onions and a couple of potatoes.

"Take this," she insisted. "And keep in touch."

He knows it will take a few days for him to pluck up the courage to go back and see them again. For now, he's heading diametrically away from his tenement room on Calzada de Monte, but he needs the pipe wrench and pliers he lent to Bienve and he'll never get them back unless he turns up at his place unannounced. Whether they have a few drinks or not, he's not leaving without his tools. No more Mr. Nice Guy. No one lends him so much as a rusty old nail when he needs it, he tells himself as he crosses the Parque La Normal.

Just at that moment, he hears a commotion coming from the other side of Manglar Street, on the corner of Árbol Seco. He is gripped by the same sense of fear and confusion that took hold of him when he jumped the fence to get out of the embassy. He's still not quite himself. Just thinking about the story he's heard gives him the jitters. His son's school friend was beaten up and lost an ear for wearing the foreign shirt and sneakers his cousin had given him before heading off for the embassy. Thank goodness Eduardo is doing his military service, away from all this madness. That's the first time Ángel has found anything positive about conscription. As for Emilia, she must be used to it by now.

Little by little, he moves unwittingly toward the tumult and manages to make out two men, backs bent, pummeling someone on the floor. A woman hovers over them, waiting to deliver a blow with a stick.

"Here's her other half!" Ángel hears a woman shout from behind him.

He suddenly finds himself being pulled by the hair and slapped at the same time. He makes a clumsy attempt to bash the woman clutching his hair with the bag of onions and potatoes. Moments later, he drops the bag to seize the arm of a boy in school uniform, locked around his neck. When he sees a man coming at him from the corner of his right eye, he kicks out to keep the man at bay.

As he battles to free himself, the local police chief arrives and shouts over and over, struggling to make himself heard, ordering the bloodthirsty crowd to release their prey.

"Leave him alone, for God's sake, he has nothing to do with it!"

Ángel has now heard Mireya's voice, and caught sight of her reddened face and teary eyes.

"Shut up, you lowlife, you're all the same, the whole bunch of you! Dirty scumbags!" a woman lashes back at her, determined to have the last word.

The mob grudgingly starts to calm down. At the risk of getting knocked over, the police chief hails a taxi, which seems reluctant to slow down, never mind pull up.

The barrage of insults is now directed at Ángel, who manages to break free and jumps out into the road. A truck brakes and skids. Ángel feels a dull blow to his left ear, followed by an uncomfortable ringing. He is still on his feet, crossing the other half of Manglar — which means, he realizes, that it was nothing worse than a well-placed punch that nearly knocked him out. He then opens the back door of the Lada into which the policeman has hurriedly shoved Mireya, and throws himself headfirst onto the seat.

The taxi driver speeds off without waiting for him to close the door.

*****

Back home, Mireya, still sore from the beating, tends to her wounds. She has no words of reproach for Ángel. On the contrary, she has just remarked on his admirable survival instinct and tells him how she and Sofía, both malnourished but with the promise they would be granted visas, finally left the embassy with their safe-conducts after ten agonizing days. She hasn't let the girl leave the house since their return, precisely for fear of an "act of repudiation" or a "lightning rally". She herself had only gone out on a couple of occasions, mainly to see her friend Ñica in Árbol Seco and get hold of some food. One couldn't be too careful.

But she wanted to take as many useful documents as possible abroad with them, like Sofía's grades from her first year of secondary school. That's why she decided to risk it and go in person that morning to Antonio Maceo High School, arriving during the second lesson in the hope that she would find someone in the administrative and head teacher's offices by then — while avoiding uncomfortable meetings in the corridors. She offered her resignation to the deputy head, who refused it, explaining that Mireya had already been dismissed from her job as a cleaning assistant on the grounds that she represented a bad example for the pupils. The woman said she was genuinely sorry for Sofía but understood Mireya's reasons for not wanting to send her to school, given the circumstances. She told her to go to the administrative office for the termination papers, but there was no one there to attend to her, so Mireya ended up leaving the school two hours later, the same way she came in: empty-handed. Then she decided to throw caution to the wind, go and see Ñica. She reached her friend's place without any sign of trouble, but a group of teachers and pupils, an advance party and another unit lying in ambush in the park, were waiting for her on the way home. The rest Ángel has seen and suffered in the flesh.

"What's that noise?" he asks her from his favorite armchair in the living room.

"I don't know. It sounds like it's coming from down there," she answers as she makes her way to the balcony.

"Hey, hey, ho, ho! Scum! Worms! Out you go! Hey, hey, ho, ho! Scum! Worms! Out you go!"

The chant is repeated over and over, like a mantra.

"Down with the worms!"

"Out with them! Out with them! Out with them!"

"Leave the girl here, you shameful mother, the poor child doesn't know what's ahead of her!"

The din of the rally resounds in the passageway.

"Oh, dear God, protect us," begs Mireya, looking out at the hostile mob through the slats of the blinds on one of the storm doors.

At that very moment, an egg breaks against the balustrade and a stone hits the window, cracking the glass.

"Move away from the balcony and take the girl into the back," says Ángel.

"Carter, loser, take your lowlifes with you! Carter, loser, take your lowlifes with you!"

"Out with them! Out with them! Out with them!"

Ángel heads down the stairs carrying a chair. He bolts the door and wedges the chair between the lock and the bottom step. He mutters under his breath, cursing the people repeating and varying their slogans as if their chants could resolve the problems of an entire lifetime and a whole country. Meanwhile, Mireya has pushed the armchairs and various other pieces of furniture against the balcony doors. Hearing her, Ángel realizes they also need to block the ones opening out onto the inner courtyard from the living room, three bedrooms and kitchen. No one can access the stairway, but they could easily get into the house through the neighbor's or from the roof terrace.

"Fidel, Fidel, give the Yankees hell! Fidel, Fidel, give the Yankees hell!"

*****

Half an hour into the siege, the insults give way to shouts of, "Long live the Revolution!" and the barrage of objects gradually wanes, the crowd finally dispersing.

Ángel wants to head back to his tenement room but Mireya insists he stay for something to eat. She serves up three egg sandwiches and a jug of banana milkshake. Sitting between the two of them at the table, Sofia observes them in turns, as if watching a tennis match. Ángel and Mireya chew their food in silence, looking at each other like the old friends they are. The act of repudiation has left them shell-shocked.

"What a crazy mob!" Mireya breaks the awkward silence. "Don't you worry, princess. You'll see how soon you forget about all this when your Yankee boyfriend takes you out in his shiny new car to Miami Beach and, there you are, with your trendy sunglasses…"

"Boyfriend? I don't want a boyfriend."

"Not now you don't, but the day you're going out with a nice, tall, blond American boy you'll remember this conversation."

"I love milkshakes," says Ángel, trying to sound cheerful. "I used to drink them till they came out of my ears when I was your age…"

As he listens to himself speak, Ángel comes to the realization that he's an outsider in that house. Even if he were to believe in Mireya's fanciful ideas about the girl's future, he knows he has no part in it. And so he limits himself to small talk and looks at Sofía, who smiles at him for a moment, then continues to slowly chew her egg sandwich. The dark circles have all but disappeared, yet her eyes are dulled by a cloud of sadness.

That Settles It

The day has come. Today, April 19, 1980, to commemorate the nineteenth anniversary of the historic Bay of Pigs victory, a giant demonstration has been planned by the

Confederation of Cuban Workers, the Federation of High School Students, the Committees for the Defense of the Revolution, and all the other seasoned mass organizations. It is estimated that more than a million Cubans will march down Fifth Avenue, in front of the Peruvian Embassy, in support of the Revolution and against imperialism and internal scum. It's the "March of the Combatant People".

Returning to his tenement room after buying the last two editions of *Granma*, croquettes, two rolls and a bottle of moonshine — he doesn't have enough for rum — Ángel finds himself at the bus stop, face to face with the president of his neighborhood Committee for the Defense of the Revolution.

"Angelito, come here a second. Man, I've been wanting to talk to you for days," the woman says to him, a lit cigarette hanging from a corner of her mouth.

Why hasn't she joined the march with everybody else? She doesn't look sick. Whatever the reason, Ángel knows he's got more to lose in this casual encounter. Of the two of them, everybody knows which one has dubious moral values. And who does the informing.

The woman, in a robe that allows him a glimpse of her breasts, bulging and freckled, draws him away from the bus stop and leads him to a corner, murmuring that there are too many gossips around. Then she tells him, speaking in a low voice but not beating about the bush, that she's well aware of what's going on with Mireya.

"We've known her for years and we know she's a good person. But the thing is, we're facing difficult times, critical times, and people are fired up. Just tell her not to leave the house and soon she'll see that she won't have any trouble."

And what will happen to me? Ángel wants to ask. But he bites his tongue. From the woman's confidential tone, he'd like to think that he won't be subjected to the people's rage, that he can continue living his life as he has until now. At least they aren't stoning him. Despite the hypocrisy that

23

could be detected in her words, he is reassured by the simple fact that they've been uttered by the president of the CDR. But it's clear that Mireya is seen as a sellout in her homeland and, given his relationship with her, he's also part of the nest of maggots, the national scum, one more anti-social element. He only hopes that his friendly face will make the woman believe that he, Ángel Ribot, remains on the straight and narrow. For now, he wants to go home and not hear or see anybody for the rest of the day.

*****

As soon as Ángel reaches his den, he goes to a corner, opens the bottle of moonshine, and tips the first bit out, just to the base of the neck. For the saints. Just in case. He barely believes in the mother who bore him, but he has overlooked this gesture more than once and the precious liquid has always spilled with some inexplicable pirouette of the bottle.

"Get off my back, for fuck's sake! Let me live!" he exclaims after a long swig from the bottle.

Then he begins to close doors and windows, both downstairs and on the makeshift mezzanine.

Downstairs again, he pours a drink into a glass and takes another gulp, sitting with the newspapers in front of him and trying to follow the tangled thread of events. The Americans are staging some "Solid Shield 80" military maneuvers in the Caribbean and landing 2000 marines at the Guantánamo naval base. A battalion of 1200 soldiers from the military will also be transported to the base. President Carter says his heart is with the asylum seekers. Yesterday's edition of *Granma* indicates the mobilization points for each municipality, the departure schedules and the concentration area assigned around Fifth Avenue. Special traffic regulations are being established on account of the march.

Ángel turns on the television and finds himself looking at thousands of people marching and shouting in unison, "Commander-in-Chief, at your service!" The second of the two channels displays a similar crowd. Many people are holding up placards that read: "The lazy ones can go! Let the antisocials go! Cuba is for people who produce!"

He pours another drink from the bottle, which has gone down by about a quarter.

According to one of the papers, El Salvador and Colombia won't accept any Cuban asylum seekers because of serious unemployment problems. The Dominican Republic won't accept any antisocial elements. Peru is talking about receiving 1000. Spain, 500. The United States, maybe 2000. Nothing is official. Canada's Chancellor denies that his country has decided to offer asylum to any of the subjects who have broken into the embassy. Not only has it not decided what kind of action to take, it hasn't even considered the question in an official capacity. For their part, the workers and militants of the People's Power in Caimanera object to people's slogans as reported in the April 20 edition of *Granma*, which included "Ping, Pong, Out, Down with Caimanera", because Caimanera is one of the most courageous municipalities in the province of Guantánamo, as well as being the first anti-imperialist trench.

Three hundred and ninety antisocial elements have left the Peruvian diplomatic headquarters and gone home. A passport and a definitive safe-conduct will be given not only to those who have entered the embassy but also to all the lowlifes requesting it. At least Alfredo will leave, taking with him the repulsive habit of putting his glass eye in his own rum tumbler. Let's see if people laugh at that up north. Goodbye and good riddance. But Mireya and Sofía will also leave with this new measure, and heaven knows who else. Ángel racks his brains for an instant, searching for things that will prove he and his children belong to the nest of maggots, the scum, which will facilitate their departure together. But it's better just to leave things as they are without complicating them further. He'll have to be careful not to step out of line, he reminds himself, so they aren't hostile toward him or his loved ones. In the end, the people who seek reprisals today are the ones who will apply to leave tomorrow. And the farce will continue just as it has for the past twenty years. A disgusting simulacrum but that's the way it is.

He takes another gulp and returns to the *Granma*.

Comparing the two copies of the paper, he observes two boxes under the title "News from Mariel", which show the number of people who left the day before and the number of boats from the United States in the Havana port at press time.

For the rest of the week, *Granma* after *Granma*, Ángel will notice that the box is either red or black, that it can appear in the bottom right or bottom left-hand side of the first or second page, square or rectangular; it can emphasize safety as a key element of the Mariel-Florida route, or include information about the weather in the straits. But it never fails to mention the number of antisocials abandoning the country and that of boats in the port of Mariel.

The official organ of the Communist Party of Cuba publishes these statistics with such regularity that Ángel decides to bet on the last two digits of the figures — like he did in 1970, betting on the tons of sugar produced in the "Ten-Million-Ton Sugar Harvest". At that time, he would look on the first page, under "Harvest Progress", line "Havana", column "Today". Now he'll have options to choose from. He could bet on the number of immigrants, on the number of boats, or both. That settles it.

In the Footsteps of Francis Drake

Bob Nash had thought he'd be able to relax in the casual ambience of his favorite bar on the shores of Safe Harbor, Stock Island, far from the Key West crowds. He gazed out at the shrimping boats as they approached and left the coast, and then sank his teeth into a piece of bread with hogfish caught by a local diver. But the radio broadcaster's voice still resounded in his ears and the words of the announcement churned feverishly in his head: a group of Cuban-Americans intended to get their boats together and sail to the territorial waters' edge to protest against Castro's emigration policy.

Within three days, this Key West-based Englishman saw eight of those boats being transported on land. According to reports on the radio, the rest approached by sea, and some refugees were saying that the island's government had opened its coasts so that anyone who wanted to leave could do so. Later, Bob saw a fishing boat and two private vessels berth in the southernmost docks of the United States with around three hundred Cubans aboard.

That same week, during a brief trip in coastal waters on his motorboat the *Lady Marion*, Bob saw a further eleven boats with over seven hundred refugees arrive. He also received, through maritime radio, instructions transmitted by the Coast Guard to the hundreds of US-based Cubans determined to bring back islanders. They were to go through Customs, respect the capacity restrictions specified in the vessels' documentation, provide a floating device for every person aboard, and immediately notify the Immigration and Naturalization Service on returning to the United States with foreigners.

This morning, once again aboard the *Lady Marion*, Bob learned that the Coast Guard air patrol had sighted some fifty boats to the south of Key West and a similar number between Miami and Fowey Rocks, all headed south. Radio waves indicated that they were bound for Cuba. Three had broken down and been towed back to land. Others had run out of fuel or anchored along the barrier reef. He saw a Coast Guard ship and an HH-52 helicopter as they patrolled the area and offered help to the boats.

Now, drinking coffee in a corner bar, the local newspaper in front of him, he watches, stunned, as dozens of recreational crafts transported on trailers line up along the streets leading to the port, waiting to be launched. He estimates that another hundred boats are being trundled around the key. There is constant activity and the bar's bewildered customers can't understand where so many sailors have come from and why no one speaks English.

Bob returns to his newspaper and re-reads that the fleet has reached a thousand boats. He has a premonition that these developments will change his life. Ever since he started sailing — years ago now, in his native Devon — he's always hoped to earn a modest fortune through his skills as a seaman. He isn't fooled by the thought that the Straits of Florida could amass him unimaginable riches in 1980. He won't make his millions on the little Cubans fleeing Castro. But he'll surely make off with his modest cut. And, to a certain extent, he'll be following in the footsteps of his countryman Francis Drake, a privateer after his slave-trafficking days.

*****

Returning from Cuba with a dozen islanders just before a minihurricane forms around midday on Sunday, April 27, Bob watches how the Coast Guard, aside from escorting and towing boats, bring the rescued people aboard. In just five minutes, the group on land and the cutters assigned to the area say they have received a torrent of calls for help. So many that it's impossible to keep an exact count.

*****

The bad weather reduces the number of departures only temporarily. In early May, an avalanche of Cuban-Americans outnumbers by far the artists and visitors on the streets of Key West. Their pockets are full of money to rent or buy boats. They're not the wealthiest Miamians, but somehow they achieve their purpose: ignoring the authorities' warnings of possible fines, confiscation and arrest, they set off in groups of twenty ships. The owners of shrimping boats and recreational crafts take advantage of the situation, charging up to a thousand dollars for each Cuban they are hired to bring to the US.

Euphoric, Bob returns from a second expedition to the island in conditions far worse than the weather forecasts had predicted: a spate of electrical storms and gusts of wind extend over the ninety miles separating the Cuban capital from the Florida Keys.

The frenzy has spread, reaching parts of the US far removed from the Caribbean. According to the news, the Coast Guard has no choice but to stop and tow all the way to Shark River Station, New Jersey, an unusable liberty launch that hasn't been registered, documented or inspected, and her operator hasn't been able to show a license. Meanwhile, an old minesweeper, chartered by a church in New Orleans, bought outright in Boston, moved to New Orleans and rechristened there, has reached Key West with over four hundred refugees.

The flow of boats continues unabated. Some four hundred leave every day from Key West alone, and the Cuban government has just announced the presence of seventeen hundred docked in Mariel port.

*****

Midday. Bound for Cuba on his third trip, Bob learns that, due to bad weather and delays in processing candidates for family reunification, some Miamians have been forced to return without their relatives. His passengers have paid him five hundred dollars for the voyage and then another thousand for each person they bring back from Cuba — up front and with no reimbursement. He sees no reason to hurry back if things get complicated in Havana. As it turned out, it was on his second return trip to the States that it got messy when, by sheer chance, he got in the way of both the port authorities and the Coast Guard. They threatened to carve "Second Timer" on the windshield, but that was all. The worst that could happen is that they'd confiscate his forty-by-twelve-foot boat, but that's very unlikely, given how busy the gringos are with so many Cubans in the straits — none with papers or any goddamn sense of how to sail. It's quite clear to him that none of his exiles, even the ones coming all the way from California, considers the possibility of returning without their people. Any difficulties should serve not as a deterrent but as an incentive to continue the enterprise.

*****

In the afternoon, with eight Cuban-born passengers and the young Puerto Rican captain Dave Marrero, Bob painstakingly enters the bay to the west of Havana. Traffic is slow and chaotic. Hundreds of boats, struggling against the waves and a wind that hints at a storm, obstruct his view of the water.

Several small boats approach from land, selling assorted goods. People aboard the *Lady Marion* complain about the exorbitant prices, suspect that the vendors are State Security agents, and discover that the Cuban government is offering credit to the boats, but won't let them leave until the debt is paid off.

"It's dangerous to use credit," Bob warns. "We have cookies, sausages and sardines. But it's better to save them for the Cubans who get out. For the kids. Don't use credit, please."

"They're not letting boats dock at the main wharf," the *Lady Marion* is informed by a shrimping boat.

"Don't believe anything they tell you and only half of what you see," Dave tells the passengers.

*****

Night falls and the weather isn't quite as bad as Bob had feared; he tries to take a nap in the cabin while on deck his clients listen to the news that some American hostages have been executed in Iran in retaliation for the Operation Eagle Claw rescue mission launched by Carter on April 24.

Suddenly, the Radio Reloj broadcaster's voice is drowned out by the sound of gunfire.

"Hey, what's that?" a passenger asks.

"They're shooting at people swimming toward the boats," someone responds from the little craft beside them.

"No way! It sounds much heavier. I'd guess it's the Coast Guard trying to impose order with artillery."

"Just you wait — a war's going to break out right here and we'll be stuck in the middle of it."

People's worries are interwoven with the darkness and the rocking of the waves. From time to time, the spotlights' frenetic movements force them to duck down, fearing a dissuasive burst of gunfire. Hours pass this way — until, around four in the morning, the *Lady Marion* receives permission to dock.

The first concrete information provided by the immigration agents is that the passengers may apply for reunification with their family on condition that fifty percent of the yacht's capacity be reserved for the asylum seekers in the Peruvian Embassy. Megaphone in hand, one of the officers comes to request the list of solicited relatives. That's when anxiety skyrockets: they haven't set foot on land, haven't made any phone calls, and don't even have anything to write with. But a stubby pencil appears over here, a sheet of paper over there, and by the time Nash resurfaces with a couple of pens and a notepad, a woman has already handed over to the soldier the names of her relatives, scribbled on a coffee filter. Another woman trembles, pen in hand, as she asks her partner what will befall her own family if she can't take them with her and they are revealed to the authorities, not to mention their neighbors, co-workers and classmates.

"I don't think you can apply for so many people, but that will be determined by a higher authority," is all the officer remarks.

Shortly after, they learn that they may go to the Tritón Hotel to rest, eat and call their families. The news reaches them like a light breeze, refreshing the atmosphere of impatience and meager information.

*****

Around six p.m. it starts to rain and various passengers aboard the *Lady Marion* are soaked in the downpour, jumping and laughing, oblivious to Fidel's speech as it filters through the loudspeakers. A few hours later, two immigration representatives come and return some of the lists, explaining that they must be reduced to three relatives per visitor.

"This is the last straw! After pawning properties and paying in advance to cross the straits!" the exiles seem to exclaim without moving their lips.

Some are already petrified by the news received by phone from their own families: the daughter of the man from Kendall is set to leave with her daughter, but her husband won't authorize the girl's departure; the nephew of the couple from Hialeah can't leave because he is a soldier and has been mobilized. Dave begins to feel an uncomfortable tension in his neck and shoulders. His eyes seek solace in Bob's, but the Englishman avoids eye contact with his captain.

Although it's already almost midnight, a few distant voices sound:

> Químbara quimbara cumbaquín bambá
> Químbara quimbara cumbaquín bambá
> Heeey, mamá
> Heeey, mamá

It's not long before the reason behind the singing reaches the *Lady Marion*. Concerned about the tense international situation, a couple in a neighboring boat decided to move their wedding date forward. There was a notary on a shrimping boat who was willing to authenticate the union. She wore a shawl lent to her by an older woman and a broad-brimmed hat belonging to another. For the photos, the bride and groom toasted with 7 Up and blew out a candle embedded in a melon. Now they're enjoying a brief honeymoon in the cabin while the characteristic percussion of a carnival troupe rings out, accompanied by a whistle and a chorus:

> I feel a bass drum. Mamita, it's calling me
> Yes, yes, it's calling me

The Goodbye

Emilia watches as Pepe paces like a rabid dog on the ground floor of the tenement unit. He seems outraged at the news: Fidel has circumvented the American embargo by stocking the ships docked at Mariel with food.

"He's just created a free zone, that son of a bitch," he finally blurts out. "Purging dissidents isn't enough for him anymore. He wants to provoke another crisis with the Americans."

"The only thing to be done with this country is leave it, once and for all," Emilia declares as she switches off the TV, which was showing a crowd with posters reading "Today, like Yesterday, United with Fidel" and "Gringos, Go Home".

"Who told you that a person could show up in Cuatro Ruedas as scum?" Pepe asks her in a near whisper. "But keep your voice down 'cause the walls here have ears and the courtyard has eyes. I don't know why that goddamn door has to be open all day long."

Emilia pulls a cigarette from the pack of Populares on top of the TV, lights it and leans briefly into the corridor of the tenement building.

"Put aside the paranoia for a second and listen to me, will you? Adrián's the latest one to confirm it, but half of Havana knows. I can't understand how you didn't find out yourself since you're so involved in politics and everything. Do me a favor and watch the rice — I'm going to the pharmacy and then to Dad's. When I get back, we'll have lunch and talk calmly about all this. Although, if it were up to me, I'd go to Cuatro Ruedas right now or wherever I have to go to get out of this place."

"Can you get some Dexedrines? The way things are looking, we're going to need more."

"By being greedy you might end up with nothing, sweetheart. You know perfectly well that pills are rationed."

"You don't have to remind me. Everything here is rationed except for disappointment and policemen."

"Fine. Get me the prescription, but make it quick."

Bending over the aluminum table under the stairs that lead to the loft, Pepe forges the writing and signature on the top sheet of a prescription pad. Meanwhile, Emilia thinks about the years of planning and dreaming that have drifted by while they waited for a moment like this. She'll wait till the very last minute to tell her father since she trusts nothing, not even the memory of her own mother. It turns out that Ángel tells Mireya everything, and the woman has already meddled in Emilia's affairs on more than one occasion. As for Eduardo, what can be done if the poor guy is in the military? The only way to help him is from up north: either applying to have him join her in the US through a family reunification process or getting him out via a third country.

Pepe approaches her with the prescription and asks for a drag of her cigarette. Exhaling the smoke through his nose, he throws an arm around her shoulders, pulls her to him and kisses her on the forehead. She shrugs him off affectionately and says from the doorway, "Look for the prison papers and the rest of your documents, and I'll be right back. Don't forget to keep an eye on the rice. Turn off the burner at twenty past and don't take off the lid."

*****

Emilia rings the bell on a door along the sidewalk of Passageway B, Arroyo Street, but no one answers. She presses the button again and waits. After turning her head and half her body, about to go, she decides to try one last time. At that very moment, the door starts to open slowly, activated by a cord that extends up the stairs inside. Emilia lets herself be swallowed into the shadows of the hall.

Upstairs now, waiting for someone to receive her, she admires the wicker armchairs beside the balcony, and the two nineteenth-century columns separating the living room from the entrance hall. Brushing the fronds of a betel palm and some xanthosoma leaves, Sofia appears through the open-air hallway. Emilia takes the little girl's face into her hands and gives her a kiss on the forehead before saying,

"Your hair looks lovely! This little vacation has been good for you."

"I'll be right there. Can I get you some coffee?" Mireya calls from the kitchen at the far end of the long hallway.

"Just a little one, thanks," Emilia responds, keeping her voice down and gesturing with her index finger and thumb.

"Why don't you go bring me the coffee your mom's making for me?" she asks the girl, stroking her hair and turning her round.

As soon as Sofia disappears, Emilia peers into the adjacent room, where she has glimpsed her father stretched out on the bed with his shoes on: an inert body enveloped in semidarkness. She had looked for him at his place after leaving the pharmacy and taking two Dexedrines. When she saw he wasn't home, she revived with a third pill and decided to try Mireya's house. And here he is. There's nothing to be gained from saying anything now, she tells herself. Silently observing his gaunt body curled up in the fetal position, she imagines his wake. A few tears spring to her eyes. She tries to banish them when she sees Mireya coming down the interior corridor.

"I can wake him up if you want," Mireya offers, handing Emilia her coffee.

"Let him sleep; he looks tired."

The two women chat standing up, cup and saucer in hand.

"They could call us at any moment," Mireya says. "I'm barely sleeping. And I shower two or three times a day. Unfortunately, your dad won't be able to keep the house, but he's taking the most valuable stuff, little by little, to sell it or take it to his place. Now that you're here, honey, do you want to take something for the two of you?"

Emilia hears the reproach in her comment and bites her lip.

"Whatever you want," Mireya continues. "If it's too big, you could come with Pepe later on. Look, this sewing machine is as good as new and it'll go to waste. Wouldn't that be a shame? If they came right now to take an inventory, nothing else could leave the house."

"Thank you, really, but we don't need anything, fortunately."

"Tell me one thing, Emilita, sweetie. Instead of waiting and waiting, why don't you and Pepe put yourselves forward as scum and take your dad with you?"

Emilia sighs. Not so long ago the constant little digs would have drawn anger from her in response. Sarcasm at the very least. Now she is just too tired for that.

"The truth is we're sick of waiting to leave on political grounds, and now everyone is leaving, as you know."

She lowers her gaze into her cup.

"If I were you, I'd show up before they change their minds and close the doors again for fear of ending up with an empty island. Never mind being hostile to the revolution. Say that Pepe's a fag and you're a dyke. That you go to orgies at Purita's and practice Santeria, or you're Jehovah's Witnesses, or whatever! Pluck his eyebrows and dye his hair with peroxide, and you dress in some tomboyish way, using one of his shirts and his big watch. Whatever it takes to get out."

She wouldn't think twice about it but Pepe wants to wait. It wasn't for nothing that he got through seven years locked up in Boniato. He doesn't like to brag about the time he served as a political prisoner, but he was among the ones who never wavered, who never accepted a rehabilitation plan or wore a regular prison uniform. Now she is supposed to suggest that he should leave like all the other riffraff? Emilia takes another sip of her coffee.

"What does Dad think about you leaving. If he'd wanted to leave, he would've gone with you to the embassy, right? Do you really think he's willing to declare himself scum?"

"Honey, don't you want me to wake him? He's napping because he helped my brother fix the car and they had a few drinks. Hold on, let me tell him you're here."

"No, don't!" Emilia grabs her arm and holds her back. "I want to talk with you first to know what you think and what I should be ready for."

"Come here for a second, sweetie. I have to tell you something."

Mireya leads Emilia down the stairs to the landing, trying to distance her from both the room where Ángel is sleeping and the living room, where Sofia rocks in a chair, her ears pricked to hear their conversation.

"Can I count on you to keep a secret?"

"What secret?"

"Promise me you won't tell anyone."

"Promise."

Mireya adopts a confidential air and glances sideways at Sofia.

"Your father did go into the embassy with us, but then he had a change of heart and left."

Emilia purses her lips and nods slightly, but she is shattered. The strength leaves her body; her knees are about to give way and she fears she might fall. What is her stepmother trying to tell her?

"I'm telling you this so you can bear it in mind, not so you'll reproach your father. And certainly not so you'll go spreading it around, which could get him in serious trouble. I think, deep down, he left the embassy because of you two, because he didn't want to abandon you. In fact, I don't just think it — I know it. You were in that house on the beach, remember? And Eduardo was in the military unit, poor thing." Her honey-colored eyes fix Emilia with a deep gaze. "The fact is, now you have the chance to decide what's best for you and the whole family. One of you has to move forward first, do you understand? I mean, I've explained all of this to him! Thousands of times!"

Emilia would never have imagined that her father would even think of leaving without telling her, without saying goodbye. Although that's exactly what she is doing.

"Oh! It's getting late…" she exclaims, her voice breaking, after taking a step back and catching sight of the clock on the wall. "I have to run home 'cause…"

The words catch in her throat and the unfinished sentence hangs there. The tears that she had successfully held back now return.

"But sweet girl…" Mireya takes Emilia's hands in her own.

"I'm sorry. This whole thing, the family separating, makes me emotional," Emilia improvises, unable to offer up the faint smile she strives for, although she notes that simply uttering the sentence has stilled her sobs and helps her regain composure. "If the departure notice comes suddenly and we can't see each other, good luck and may God be with you. It's better if I don't say goodbye to Sofía. Kisses."

*****

Pepe has gathered the most important documents and put what little money he had in the house into his wallet; he takes a break, sitting down before the piles of books that are stacked on the aluminum table against the wall.

The similarity between what's happening now and what happened in '65 is obvious to him. How is it possible that Carter can't see it? Haven't the Americans learned anything from Camarioca? In the early '60s, Cubans could leave the country freely and departed by the thousands — but during the Cuban Missile Crisis of '62, Kennedy suspended the three daily flights between Cuba and the United States, stranding many people on the island who had wanted to leave. Until, in '65, Castro equipped Camarioca port so that Cubans with family in Florida could tell their relatives to come for them by sea. President Johnson never suspected that the number of refugees could become a problem when he said, at the foot of the Statue of Liberty, that Cubans seeking refuge in the US would find a safe haven there. Now, like Johnson, Carter has begun with a defiant discourse, reaffirming an arms-wide-open policy for Cubans choosing to flee their country. Who knows whether he'll maintain this stance when he's hit with a large wave? Pepe hasn't forgotten that Johnson was forced to request Castro's help in order to end the resulting migration crisis. As Emilia said, Camarioca is irrefutable proof that Fidel can open the borders whenever he wants to release internal pressure and cleanse the island of dissidents. Haven't the Americans learned their lesson?

"You can't make brains appear where there aren't any to be found! These Americans never learn!" he says to himself, somewhere between perplexed and disappointed, opening his eyes wide and shaking his head from side to side.

He can't believe it: he's just caught himself gesturing like the Tyrannosaurus himself. All he needs now is to lift his arms and repeatedly touch his temples. He imagines his sworn enemy stroking his beard and walking from one end to the other of his office on the Plaza de la Revolución, skirting the desk, placing one hand on the chair, and passing the other across a shelf in the bookcase topped with two small busts: one of Martí, the other of Napoleon. The despot would make a fist and extend his index finger to point at his interlocutors, who would sink into their seats as he lectured them with his most dramatic flourishes:

"We have to show the Yanks again how easily their migratory policy gets thrown into chaos. And, yes, our problems are also theirs, since they were the ones who created them in the first place. We'll see whether the American borders are controlled from Washington or from here. Once again, the Yankees will end up devouring the feast of their own ignorance, arrogance and stubbornness."

Pepe is so absorbed in his daydream that he hasn't seen or heard Emilia return. The room smells of burned rice.

Cuatro Ruedas - El Mosquito - Mariel

On the afternoon of May 8, Emilia and Pepe join the diverse group of dissidents entering what has come to be called "the scum office" in Cuatro Ruedas: a vacant lot fenced in by seven-foot-high boards. They are met with insults and aggression from both sides.

Inside, the bureaucracy imposed by the authorities means that the lines barely advance. The air is filled with uncertainty, distrust and fear.

At nightfall, Pepe tells Emilia that the process will surely start to speed up at any moment; after all, even bureaucrats need to sleep, and before going home they have to finish their work. But this naïve hope vanishes when the couple sees that some of the officials seated at the reception desk are matter-of-factly replaced by others.

While their line inches forward, Pepe and Emilia are forced to remain on their feet all night long. Worn out, drowsy and with aching legs, they finally appear before an immigration agent around seven a.m.

"Criminal record?" the man asks in an apathetic tone. He has an underbite and his cheeks hang loosely off his face, as flaccid as a dog's.

"Political prisoner," Pepe responds.

"What about her?"

"She's my wife. She's against the process, too, and has as many reasons as I do for leaving."

"Your wife. OK. Have you brought your sentence and parole letter?"

"Here's everything you need," says Pepe, laying some papers on the table.

"All I need is what I'm asking you for."

Fighting his nerves and weariness, Pepe finds the two documents and places them in the man's hands without a word. On the other side of the table, the officer starts to read one of them aloud, then abruptly stops.

"What else, other than counterrevolutionary? Homosexual? Thief? Santero? Jehovah's Witness?"

Pepe limits himself to a silent shake of his head.

"We're both Jehovah's Witnesses," says Emilia out of nowhere, and wonders whether the officer will accept their case as a couple, whether he'll interrogate her separately, or try to publicly humiliate them.

Meanwhile, at the table to their left, a thin blond man addresses his interrogator, describing the minutiae of the many robberies he's participated in: places, dates, items, quantities, accomplices. On their right, a man in his fifties, who has apparently claimed to be homosexual, is ordered by two female officers to touch the buttocks of a young mulatto with an exaggeratedly effeminate manner standing beside him.

"Just tell us: are you a top or a bottom?" one of the women asks.

The man remains impassive for a few seconds. Then he grabs a buttock and squeezes.

"Boy! You'd never know it, but he's a wild one. Just look at this! I'm sure he's given me a bruise. I want to get to Gringolandia in one piece — Broadway is waiting for me."

"It's one thing to be a faggot and another to have no dignity at all. Go, get into that line over there," the woman orders the young man, stifling her laughter.

"New York, New York!" he sings as he walks away.

"As for you, you cheap old pansy, go get behind your girlyman, since you like his ass so much. Before we change our minds and throw you to a group where they'll eat you like piranhas."

"Leave your ID cards in the bucket and get in line behind those two for fingerprinting," the officer facing Emilia and Pepe finally barks after making them sign the forms he's been filling out.

After getting their fingerprints taken, they are told to wait with a group of people at the front door of a Girón bus.

When she overhears some of the others say they've been waiting for over two days in that pigsty of a place, Emilia can only attribute the speed of their own process to Pepe's political background. For an instant, she's tempted to tell her husband that Ángel had entered and left the embassy while they were away at the beach. Why should she remain silent? She had made a promise to Mireya but surely she would have already shouted the whole thing from the rooftops. There's no such thing as a two-person secret. It would have been better kept if Mireya hadn't let it out in the first place. Some favor she's done for Emilia! A family secret is too heavy a burden for her small shoulders. The longer she withholds the news from Pepe, the less she'll deserve his trust. She is now the one who has to bear the cursed cross!

Not far from the bus, beside the barracks that serve as an office, two men get out of a tanker truck. One immediately begins to unroll a hose and, after straightening out the kinks, shouts for his partner to start up the pump. As soon as he hears the engine, the man aims the nozzle at the group waiting alongside the bus. It takes only a few seconds for the jet of water to take down a couple of people before shifting to some fiber cement tanks.

The short-haired female officer who led them there has reappeared from behind the bus.

"Don't complain — it's to avoid epidemics."

The woman raps on the windshield and signals to the driver and another man in an olive-green uniform, who are chatting inside the vehicle with the doors and windows shut.

"Come on! Get in! Faster!" she then orders the group although they can only press together because the door is still closed.

As soon as they are able, many soaked and some injured, the aspiring passengers get on the bus and settle in. Almost immediately, they're off on their way.

With the boarded fence at the exit barely behind them, Emilia hears a sudden noise followed by screams. Someone on the street has thrown an egg at them. Luckily, it has smashed against a column. But several people have been splattered. Passengers rush to shut the few still-open windows before a crowd waiting beside the road begin to hurl rocks at them. Some throw themselves to the floor. Emilia ducks down.

"Easy now, the danger's over," the driver says into the rear-view mirror once the bus is moving along at a steady speed.

When most of the passengers are calmer, the second soldier gets to his feet and projects his voice all the way to the back.

"Where we're headed, they're going to take all your money from you so, if you want to leave something with us, you can give it to me now."

At that moment, the bus turns a corner and advances along an unpaved road, which every now and then bumps the chassis. Cap outstretched, the man moves down the aisle, looking the passengers in the eyes. They look back, incredulous — but also aware that they've just heard the miserable truth. After walking back up the aisle amid heavy silence and emptying the cap of its contents, the man yells once again.

"Remember the number of the bus; you'll need it when they call you. 214. Two, one, four."

*****

They come to a stop along a promontory where as many buses leave as arrive, with all their seats occupied and no one standing. Unlike Cuatro Ruedas, there are no mobs waiting at the entrance and Emilia can smell the sea.

"El Mosquito Camp. Everyone off here," the driver announces.

Leading them to a hut, men and women in customs uniforms order them to drop their money into a cardboard box. They register the arrivals and confiscate watches, jewelry, keys, wallets and all contact information for other people. Next, each is given a numbered letter of safe conduct and instructions on how, upon reaching the United States, they must claim to be asylum seekers in the Peruvian Embassy; otherwise, they won't be accepted. Finally, they are told to look for a spot to wait outside the hut.

But space is hardly abundant in this new confinement arranged along a rocky crag: over a thousand people are packed together like sardines in a tin. As she makes her way through the place with Pepe, Emilia makes a mental inventory of what she sees: a couple of grape plants, several tents, and barbed-wire fences designed to divide the space into sections for embassy asylum seekers, people engaged in the US family reunification process, political prisoners and ordinary prisoners. Everyone is jumbled together, wandering through the camp as they wait to be called, and some say they've been there for five days. She can finally see the ocean: there's not a ship in sight as the sun begins to set.

At one end of the bluff, people line up along a muddy, rocky outcrop and lower their faces to the sharp surface to drink from a water tap at ground level. Close to the drinking point, soldiers have mounted an enormous cooking pot on cement blocks around a wood fire. They stir rice, water and several dozen eggs. They serve up the concoction and a boiled egg in its shell into the hands of people passing by — like Emilia and Pepe, who eat the soupy rice and peel the eggs as they continue moving through the camp. Even though the soldiers have scattered sawdust on the spot where people relieve themselves in plain view, the stench of urine and excrement is unbearable.

The couple makes it through the night, between the reef and the tent. Around four in the morning, flashlight beams and the sound of boots treading the mud keep Emilia from sleeping. Armed with AKM machine guns, the soldiers unleash German Shepherds. They don't bite, but they make people flee in terror, fall and hurt themselves on the rocks. Emilia presses against Pepe. In front of her, two young men seated back-to-back, apparently overcome with exhaustion, don't hear the stampede — until a restless, wet nose starts sniffing at one of the men's shoes, then nudges at his ankle. The animal receives a sharp kick in the jaw and lets out a plaintive yelp, moving away with its tail between its legs.

"What happened to that dog?" a soldier barks.

No answer. Indifferent to fear, if not to caution, two shadows slip through the crowd and melt into it as if they had never existed.

*****

The afternoon languishes without the couple detecting any progress at all.

"Anyone falling asleep and not claiming their bus number loses their chance to leave. Do you hear me? Pay attention. No complaints or objections here."

The soldier who has just made this announcement begins to chant first names and the first of people's two surnames. Applicants have to respond with their second surname; if they don't, they miss out on their bus as well as their opportunity to emigrate.

Looks like we'd better get organized, Pepe tells himself, as the second night draws in over El Mosquito. He forms a group with four others in the tent and they set out to memorize the number of everyone's bus so they can alert one another if they hear their bus departures being called.

The plan bears fruit: just before three in the morning, he's awakened by voices.

He sits bolt upright and shakes Emilia. They run for the buses, shouting:

"Here, José Antonio Galán Brito and Emilia Ribot!"

"Emilia Ribot Hernández!"

In the darkness, they are led with thirty others to an abandoned swimming pool. They are ordered to file down into one end and wade to the other through stagnant water, two feet deep in the middle and littered with rotted leaves. Once the ritual with the fetid water is over, they are led to the bus area again, where, standing on the running board of a front door, a copper-skinned officer struggles to read the names of the people who are supposed to board.

Taking advantage of the confusion swirling around the list as it's read, about a dozen of the people piled up at the door manage to slip into the bus within a matter of seconds.

"Everyone stop right there! Only the ones I call are leaving! And don't get rowdy, because I'll beat the shit out of any one of you without a second thought!" the soldier shouts, dealing out a couple of kicks.

By the time the man restores order, Emilia and Pepe have shoved their way onto the bus and quickly move down the aisle, as the first rows of seats are already taken. She settles in at the back but he can't find a place. Emilia's gaze shifts from the soldier's head to those of the other seated passengers. Would it really be so hard to organize all of this in such a way that only the ones who've arrived together — whose names are on the list still clutched in the man's hand — could get on?

"Anyone who can't find a seat has to get off and board another bus," the officer shouts, looking toward the back and beginning to count heads.

The bus reeks of the water from the farewell hurdle pool. Emilia and Pepe lock eyes for an instant and he shrugs his shoulders. She continues glancing desperately in all directions but she can't find a single space for him. Just then, someone elbows her in the right side of her ribcage. Fearful, she turns her eyes in the direction of the nudge. She can't fully make out the man's gray-haired head, a hand's length away from hers. All she sees is a gold tooth whispering:

"Tell him to sit on the floor between us and to keep his head down."

*****

The bus leaves them at the entrance of Mariel port, guarded by armed soldiers. Two of them make the group line up in single file and lead them to a warehouse-like structure with wooden benches oriented toward the dock. They are made to sit in the rows furthest from the sea and told that they must move up to the seats in front of them as they are vacated.

Having advanced half the rows of benches, Emilia watches part of a boat jam-packed with people, their legs hanging from the roof and masts. Pepe signals that it's their turn to move forward, but an officer orders them to stay where they are and directs a group of men to the vacated bench in front of them. Some of the new arrivals talk to themselves; others drool. It won't be the only time they are held back before reaching the front row.

They don't go directly to the boat from the benches but are made to wait at the dock, standing lined up in tight rows under the blazing sun.

48

"Give me five more and make it fast!" Emilia hears someone shout from a mooring.

"Is it just you and your kids? No one else?" she urgently asks the young woman in front of her, who clutches a six-year-old boy with one hand and a small girl who can't be older than three with the other.

"Yes. Why?"

"Five over here! There are five of us!" Emilia shouts with all her strength, jumping up and waving her hand so they can see her.

The officer responsible for forming the lines impatiently summons them over to his partner on the yacht he's gesturing to.

"The doll!" yell people from the lines.

The mother turns her head for an instant. When she doesn't see the tiny human figure, she tells her daughter to keep running toward the pier. As they rush forward, a projectile sails through the air, launched from the dock in a perfect parabola, until it falls into the outstretched hands of a passenger on the *Lady Marion*. People applaud, both on deck and on land, and the doll passes from one hand to the next until it reaches the girl.

"Congratulations! You couldn't have asked for a better gift today," Pepe tells the woman, smiling, as they settle in to the right of the prow.

"Thank you," she replies, only then realizing that it's the second Sunday in May: Mother's Day.

The young woman pulls her son and daughter close to her, aware that, amongst the passengers, there are bound to be mothers who won't receive their children's affection today — and children who may never see their mothers again.

*****

The *Lady Marion* has to wait. No one can leave the port until the authorities have granted all due permits. As the hours pass, despite a general reluctance toward the "so-tell-me-about-yourself" dynamic, conversation has started to flow between the Cubans from the island and those in exile. Emilia speaks with a fifty-something-year-old woman whose hair is tied back with a kerchief and whose eyes gleam sharply. She says she's come for her mother, as her father died in Cuba several years prior.

"I'm sorry, what did you say your name was?" Pepe asks, joining the conversation.

"Carmen. A pleasure to meet you."

"José Antonio. The pleasure is mine." Pepe shakes the hand offered to him and continues, "Carmen, you were telling my wife that after the Cuban Missile Crisis lots of families found themselves on opposite sides of the straits. What were things like before flights were suspended? Could anyone leave who wanted to?

"But, Pepe, maybe Carmen doesn't want..." Emilia admonishes him.

"No, no." The woman raises and lowers her hand as if to clear the air. "It's fine for him to ask. It doesn't bother me. Look, between '59 and '62, the number of Cubans living in Florida rose to a quarter of a million. That figure gives you an idea of how popular the new government was by then. But it's nothing like the situation today. This is a scandal for the communists, a total disgrace."

"And Camarioca?"

"The first time they opened up. Yes, sir. Lots of ships came to Cuba from the US and they brought thousands of people back with them but, believe me, it was nothing like this."

"So you got out when the people leaving were politicians, lawyers, doctors and businessmen. The golden age of exile, right? Tell us about those days, Carmen, to entertain ourselves while we wait."

"Hey, is this some kind of interview?" Emilia protests, giving her husband a jab with her elbow.

Carmen smiles, willing to keep talking.

"A resettlement agency found us housing and work in Miami as soon as we arrived. There were also English classes, university loans, and all kinds of assistance for becoming residents and citizens. It's not the same anymore but don't you worry about what you're leaving behind — up north you'll be able to achieve what you want if you're willing to work hard."

"Up north and everywhere else that isn't here," Pepe mutters. "This country is hopeless. Have you heard the joke about the CIA agent they send to Cuba to investigate why Fidel hasn't fallen?"

"No, dear. Why don't you tell it to me?"

"So, it turns out that, after spending months on the island, observing and analyzing everything, it's finally time for the guy to write his report, and he writes: 'The situation is a complex one. There is no unemployment but no one works. No one works but all productive goals are met. All productive goals are met but the stores are empty. The stores are empty but the Cubans make do. The Cubans make do but they protest constantly. They protest constantly but then they go to the Plaza de la Revolución and applaud Fidel. They applaud Fidel but then they spend the whole day wishing he were dead.'"

"That's great! I'd like to be able to retell it but it's a little complicated, isn't it?"

"Just like life here, really. We…"

"That one! That one, there!" shouts a woman.

Two men seize a guy and wrench the jacket he's wearing off his back before hurling him to the ground and tying him to the base of a seat with a belt.

"It's a real shame that they're loading this lovely, clean yacht with lowlifes. Poor captain," Carmen says in a low voice. "As far as I know, those men with tight, garish shirts have nothing to do with those of us who've paid to come."

"You can tell from miles away they're crazy guys and common prisoners," butts in the woman who shouted before. "The one who stole the jacket was asking when the doctor was going to see him. And take a look at that other guy, the bald, barefoot one. He says they threatened to double his sentence if he didn't go."

Emilia pulls back her foot so that one of the men they are talking about can pass. Silently, she takes in the lack of space, the anxious and haggard faces around her. She then presses her back against the bow rail, craning her neck in the hope of catching a glimpse of her father and brother on land.

*****

Still without permission to leave the port, Bob Nash observes how the conditions at Mariel have worsened since the last trip — to the point where it looks like a floating concentration camp. One of the officers has just brought him twenty-five more people. After reducing the number of boats due to bad weather, it was to be expected that the government would take advantage of the situation and stick as many people as they possibly could on the boats that did leave, but this guard in particular seems determined to overload the *Lady Marion*. Doesn't he see that not one more person will fit? Is he crazy or just a total son of a bitch?

"You can't put another twenty-five on here, for God's sake! The boat will sink!" Nash gestures wildly, trying to make him understand.

"No problem. All Cubans will stay here."

"Sir, you have to understand…" Dave says.

"So get them off. Come on."

"But…" the Cubans protest in unison.

"But nothing. The individuals claimed by each boat haven't even been processed yet," the officer explains, his eyes fixed on Dave as if the others didn't exist. "You have to cooperate and take the people who are ready to depart. There are no privileges here. Family members requested for reunification will leave on other yachts, which are docked or about to arrive. If the passengers on this boat already applied for their people, they can relax because they'll be out sooner rather than later. What we're doing here right now, though, is wasting time and holding everything up."

The emigrants turn to Bob, their eyes the size of saucers, as if asking him in unison whether the yacht will make it back to Florida with this new cargo.

"All right. Fine. It's not the right thing to do, but what other choice do we have?"

And in this way, a week after its third trip to Mariel and with a hundred people on board, the *Lady Marion* joins the constant flow of little boats heading out of the harbor. Bob, retreating from the hubbub, unwraps four new life jackets — which, along with the ones available in different spots around the ship, total less than a dozen.

The Crossing

As soon as the sun goes down, it begins to thunder and the sea churns. Hundreds of vessels of all sizes come together to form an impressive flotilla. Shouted rumors leap from one to the next, and the passengers on the *Lady Marion* learn that a shrimping boat has gone down.

The news doesn't surprise Emilia, who can see how the waves rise above the defenseless little crafts. Sometimes the smallest ones disappear entirely before emerging again a few moments later. It all happens in an instant, but the anxiety to know if they will reappear is so great that she prefers not to look. Clutching the railing that surrounds the deck, she hears the roar of the motor. She supposes that the poor weather and excessive load keep it from operating at its full capacity. The sounds of their arduous progress envelop her yearning to arrive, to call her father and tell him the news, while the breeze sweeps her thick, curly hair across her eyes.

"I don't want anyone standing up, please. No one standing up, please," Bob calls out.

Sitting down, the lack of space forces Emilia to draw her knees up close to her. Her lower body registers the waves' impact on the hull, and her trembling form contracts with every lurch. In the darkness, as she prays that the boat won't break apart, she glances sideways at the fearful faces outlined against surfaces of phantasmagorical white. Most are men. Some with several-day-old beards, exhausted, injured, splattered with egg or mud. Others have shaved heads, and are trying to sleep, or crawling and slipping around, defying what increasingly resembles a gale. They have always lived on an island but for most this is their first boat trip. If their movements were clumsy before they set out, now — with the constant jolts and a prow that alternately points toward the darkened sky and plunges downward, provoking a shock each time — it's hardly surprising that they are all dizzy and vomiting. The spasms passing through a young man's body toss out what little he must have had in his belly. Emilia is struck by an urge to retch, but she resists and suppresses her nausea.

Not far from the *Lady Marion*, the *Sea Hunter*, twenty-four feet long and overburdened with migrants, floats adrift. The similarly sized *Mandy*, also drifting, is taking on water and has been evacuated. Fortunately, the American coast guards reduce the human cargo on the struggling vessels. The *Dallas*, for example, has 260 refugees on board and is towing six other boats with a further hundred people. The *Diligence*, which has just rescued all twenty-eight on board one sinking boat, escorts a convoy of another twenty-three vessels transporting around fifteen hundred people. Another ship, the *Courageous*, which has about two hundred refugees aboard, is towing several other boats.

The coast guards aren't the only ones offering assistance to boats in trouble. The *Lady Marion*, too, pulls along a 15-passenger dinghy that has run out of fuel.

*****

Around five in the morning, a sudden downpour calms the sea, instantly soaks the passengers of the *Lady Marion* and cleans the deck of vomit. An American ship approaches on the starboard side, its crew tossing lifejackets to the towed dinghy and some large bags containing sandwiches and bottles of water to Bob's yacht.

Dave, who has made his way to the stern, discreetly hands a knife to the man from Kendall and says, "If you see the dinghy starting to sink, cut the rope in time or we're all going down with her."

The man nods and winks in complicity.

"Keep going! Keep going!" come the voices from the American ship.

A helicopter hovers above them. Bob and Dave signal that everything is fine. The helicopter continues to linger overhead, its noise deafening, until the Cuban coast guards' gunboat which has approached on the port side turns around and heads back toward the island.

From the towed dinghy, a man yells, "Try to fuck with us now, cowards! Bastards!"

"Assholes!" add several passengers on the *Lady Marion*.

"Down with Fidel!"

*****

The sky's monochrome monotony has shifted from black to leaden blue, and a single gray streak lightens the sea toward the east.

"That's Key West. Fucking US of A," Dave announces, euphoric.

His comment raises the spirits of everyone on board, although no one can make out anything in that direction. Emilia eagerly looks for the outlines of skyscrapers and it takes her a while to finally glimpse a tiny dot on the horizon.

The dot disappears every now and then, as if it were a mirage. Little by little, it takes on the form of a short sideways brush stroke, but the elation fades when no major change can be detected on the skyline. Atop what looks like a church steeple, the only thing that changes is the color of the sky, from gray to a warm pink.

*****

A new dawn and an intense sun shines over a uniformly clear blue sky. Although their forward progress has been more apparent over the past half hour, the captain of the *Lady Marion*, instead of berthing at the first wharf or approaching any docking spot along the shore, even if it's a mangrove swamp, has now spent some time keeping the boat at a cautious distance from the coast. In an attempt to calm her nerves, Emilia tells herself that at least the dizziness and nausea have dissipated, and that these sensations will be forgotten altogether when she sets foot on American soil.

Suddenly, she hears applause and women shouting. Someone has just dived into the water and another young man follows the swimmer's example. Emilia's eyes search Pepe's. Without a word, they clasp hands and remain motionless.

*****

The *Lady Marion* has left behind a long line of boats waiting to dock. Shortly after nine in the morning on May 17, 1980, she berths at the Truman Annex dock in Key West.

"There's no way I'm getting down from here. That guard is going to put us all in jail," says an older woman when she sees a soldier in combat attire approaching the vessel.

"Ma'am, you're in the land of freedom now. Forget your fear and caution," encourages a man in a rayon shirt with a blue, red and green amoeba pattern.

As if to prove his point, the man takes a jubilant leap to the dock, crouches down, places his palms on the ground, and repeatedly kisses the concrete.

"Freedom! Freedom!" others exclaim as soon as their feet touch land.

From the dock, a representative of the Phillip Morris Tobacco Company reaches out to the *Lady Marion*, several packs of Marlboros in hand. The woman smiles as a kneeling photographer captures the images of Cubans gratefully accepting the cigarettes.

"They're giving out free Marlboros!"

Hearing this, about ten islanders run from port to starboard — which means that the boat nearly turns over and the Americans have to jump back, turning as pale and stiff as a pair of candles.

"Have you seen the refrigerators full of food for us?" asks one of the men still on board, gesturing toward a group of porta-potties. "Look how people go in, eat, and come back out satisfied."

"Buddy, don't mess with me. I may be from the countryside, but I'm not some stupid farmer," another man with a shaved head responds, not even glancing at the other, and getting in front of him in the line to disembark.

Not far from the washrooms, their pockets full of cigarettes, six new arrivals — all wearing the same loud, wrinkled shirts — enter a container where they've been told they can make use of clothing donated by Cuban residents. Behind a fence, a sea of people clap and shout as immigration agents lead the islanders toward the air-sea station.

After being welcomed with a can of Coke and an apple, they are transported by bus from the station to the Orange Bowl Stadium, where they spend the night before moving on to Opa-locka Airport.

In the airport, they are processed in an orderly way. The officers seem kind and even impressed by some of the refugees' educational and professional experience. When the Cubans try to address them in English, they are appreciative but insist on using Spanish. Nevertheless, Emilia notes the Americans seem curt, or apprehensive, or something of the sort. She sees it in the quick glances of their sharp eyes, in the nearly imperceptible movements across their foreheads and between their brows. Since she has no way of knowing the reason behind what may well be a product of her own paranoia, she stops worrying. She is certain she will soon recover from the Stygian crossing in this other world offering her cigarettes, Coca-Cola, apples and plentiful resources as soon as she comes to inhabit it.

A few days later, in an English-language newspaper she is to find in a laundromat, Emilia will learn that she has arrived on American soil at the same time as a curfew is imposed over Miami and four thousand police troops, summoned from all over the state, have cordoned off the black neighborhoods. African Americans have been setting vehicles, businesses and buildings on fire, protesting against the recent acquittal of four white policemen who, in December '79, had beaten a black insurance agent to death for a traffic violation. In addition to the curfew and reinforced security staff, the sale of alcohol and weapons has been temporarily prohibited.

Operation Departure

The doorbell rings. Mireya lowers the volume on the TV and leans out from the balcony: she sees two soldiers at her door.

"Mireya González Pulido?" one of the men asks.

"That's me. Just a moment. I'll be right down."

She finds it strange that they've come on foot: she's been told that summons to leave the country are usually carried out by officers from the Ministry of the Interior who arrive on motorcycles. There's just one way to prove who they are and what they want, she says to herself, as she makes her way downstairs. All those sleepless nights spent listening for the sound of a motorcycle! All the times she's run to the balcony, convinced that she's heard one! All of that, just so these two can show up on foot at ten o'clock at night, right when she's sitting down to watch television!

"Immigration," she hears as soon as she opens the door. "Is your daughter home?"

"Good evening. Why do you ask?"

"Answer the question, ma'am. Is your daughter with you or not?"

Mireya senses her neighbors watching through the slits downstairs and on the balconies. It's better that way, she thinks. Let them watch what they want, as long as it's from their own houses.

"Can't you tell me what this is about so I can..."

"Let us in if you don't want to attract the neighbors' attention."

"Come in, then."

"Bring me your ID card, the girl's minor card, and the letter of safe conduct you were given at the embassy. You have ten minutes to get out. You can't take anything with you besides your passports and the letters of safe conduct. And bring us the keys to the house. Our colleagues will be coming by shortly to seal it off."

It's the moment of truth, and she does have doubts, but the speed of the operation is enough for her to reaffirm her desire to leave. There's no time to lose and no need to exasperate the officers, she reminds herself, as she goes into Sofia's room. Her daughter is sleeping peacefully. Mireya gazes at her for a moment. There's no future in Cuba, she says silently. Then she strokes her gently and whispers into her ear that it's time, that she has to get dressed.

"Do you have everything? Follow me. I'll be taking you to the airport," the other soldier says, looking down the stairs.

Mireya gathers the little girl into her arms, gives her a kiss and goes out into the passageway at a near run, between the two men. This departure operation — which she had always imagined as a joyous moment, one in which she'd take a deep breath and surrender completely to her longed-for freedom — feels more like a humiliating raid; so much so that she fears they'll handcuff her.

The bus, which has been waiting with the engine running on the main road, lurches into movement as soon as they get in. It is then that Mireya realizes that she's leaving with only the clothes on her back, along with the desire to get on in the world and find a better future for her daughter. She's just a step away from the liberty she has yearned for.

The other steps follow in quick succession within just a few hours, after which mother and daughter find themselves in a makeshift refugee camp in the Parque Túpac Amaru, in the San Luis district of the Peruvian capital. There they encounter a few hundred other Cubans, a figure that will rise over the coming weeks.

Verdi

It starts to drizzle and Ángel decides to return to his room. After knocking on the doors of a dozen acquaintances, he hasn't managed to sell either the mixer or the wall clock he's carrying in his bag. He had hoped to make a little extra money off the clothes and objects he was able to salvage from Mireya's house, but it's turning out to be harder than he had thought.

Fina greets him at the entrance of the tenement building beside the Alborada store, asks him for a cigarette, and rejects his offerings one by one.

"You don't still have that porcelain cat, do you? You know, the one I always admired at your apartment in Ayestarán," she says.

When she mentions the figurine, Ángel recalls Fina and Hilda's daily escapes from the El Miño sausage factory so they could have a quick coffee in the apartment where he and Hilda lived at the time. Before he can respond, he takes a moment to untie the knot forming in his throat as he remembers the affection they'd professed for each other and the family they had started there.

"Yeah, I still have it. It's yours for sixty pesos, as long as it doesn't end up in the hands of a stranger. The truth is you'd be getting me out of a jam, and you'd end up with an object easily worth three hundred. I bet you didn't know that my old mother-in-law often used to take it with her to the opera at weekends. It's a very cultured cat, you know that? His name's Verdi, but you can call him whatever you want; the poor guy has probably forgotten his own name, considering all the time he's been collecting dust in a corner."

"Oh, Angelito, forget the cat's name and get down to business. I can give you twenty-five pesos for it if you bring it to my house while I've got the money, before I spend it on food."

"Goddammit, Fina, be reasonable."

"Thirty."

"Let's say fifty and call it a deal. I have to eat, too."

"Let's meet in the middle. Forty. Okay? I want us to help each other out, like the good friends we are."

"All right then. Deal. Don't move. I'll be back with the cat in under an hour."

*****

Ángel sets the heavy bag onto the table and climbs up to the wooden loft. His soul has returned to his body. He dries and combs his hair in the tiny bathroom, pulls on a raincoat over his wet clothes and takes the Chinese porcelain figurine from the shelf. Before going back downstairs, he checks he can conceal the object under the coat.

He doesn't notice how, with every step, the cat slides a little further down beneath the nylon until it brushes his thigh, slips out onto one of the wooden steps, bounces onto the next, still intact, and finally shatters into a million pieces on the tiled floor.

Ángel remains motionless for an instant, then lets his body drop. He sits on the stairs, as pale as the porcelain shards. He decides not to get up until he has made it up to Hilda for his mean-spirited action. So many tiny, endless, fruitless battles have him penned in, confronting everyone — at this point, even the dead. Despite all his efforts, the hardships increase and the fence keeps closing in on him...

He hears a knock, but he stays on the stairs, silent. He's in no shape to open the door. He doesn't want to see anyone.

"Ángel. It's Migue."

The last straw in this losing streak is that even the bets have been stalled ever since the neighborhood's two legmen left the country. Luckily, Chico and Migue liked his idea of betting on the numbers reported in *Granma*, which would let them dispense with both the Venezuelan radio station and the legman — not to mention the bank itself. Since the numbers are published in the paper, they will all be able to check them. To avoid depending on the bank, each of them should bet five pesos on the last digit of the emigration figure, and five on the last digit of the number of boats docked in Mariel. If no one is right, no one loses; if one of the three wins, the two losers have to hand over their five pesos. If two bet on the same number and win, they share what the loser has bet. The arrangement also takes weekends into account: since *Granma* isn't published on Sundays, the Saturday and Sunday bets are made against the figures that appear in the Monday edition. It's a brilliant system, he congratulates himself.

"Ángel!"

What's even better, though, is the offer he's accepted from his brother-in-law Perico to become a collector, the one who gathers the money and pays the legmen. The opportunities for promotion are ideal, since the network needs someone for the area between Carraguao and El Canal, and the bank happens to be Mireya's brother. He'll run higher risks, but the money will be better. It will also be guaranteed, no matter who wins or who loses.

"Coming!" he finally calls, now convinced that seeing a friend will lift his spirits.

No one can know about his becoming the collector, not even Migue. At least not for now. Ángel will tell him later, when he's properly settled in the post. "I've had to work quietly and somewhat indirectly, because, to achieve certain objectives, they must be kept under cover," he thinks, quoting from memory one of Martí's phrases, made popular by a TV series about superheroes in the State Security forces.

Seal

Ángel, Chicho and Migue bet on the *Granma* numbers for the first time on Tuesday, May 6, a day on which 3308 "antisocial elements" leave the country and 1477 vessels are docked at Mariel port, arriving from Florida. Migue wins for the number of emigrants, which means that Ángel and Chico have to hand over five pesos each. None of them correctly guesses the number of boats.

Wednesday, May 7: 4033 antisocial elements, 1404 boats. No one wins or loses.

Thursday, May 8: Ángel wins with 3068 elements.

Friday, May 9: He doesn't win, but he doesn't lose either.

Saturday, May 10: He wins again and buys some sausages from an old acquaintance who steals them from El Miño.

Monday, May 12: He loses.

Tuesday, May 13, a day of bad luck: Due to unpredictable weather, not a single antisocial element can leave the country for the United States. *Granma* extols the route's prestige and announces that 1275 boats remain in the port. Following a discussion about the implications of these unexpected circumstances for their arrangement, the three friends decide to cancel their bets for the day.

Wednesday, May 14: 4388, 1272. Ángel loses.

Thursday, May 15: No one wins and the betting is threatened by President Carter's order that all trips from

Florida to Mariel be suspended and that the boats docked at the Cuban port must return empty to the United States.

That Thursday, Ángel realizes he hasn't heard anything from his children for around a week. He has no way of knowing whether Eduardo has been denied a pass for some kind of misdemeanor, but at least he can visit Emilia at her room on Zequeira Street to see how she's doing. And so he sets out in that direction.

Uncertainty and fear of possible reprisals consume him, even though he hasn't yet detected any signs that people know about his seeking asylum. He worries about Eduardo or Emilia undergoing the same experience as his neighbor, Juan, who was fired from his job and beset with various acts of repudiation merely because his brother had sought asylum in the embassy. To top it off, the police visited the poor man not long ago and told him he'd have to find work or they would enforce the "vagrant's law" against him. And if the only available work is hunting crocodiles in the Zapata swamp? Even garbage collecting is run by State Security! What kind of work could Emilia find as a teacher of Literature who's been unemployed for years because of her marriage to a former political prisoner?

Despite the fact that his daughter's street seems calm, Ángel feels the target of inhibiting, paralyzing stares. He defies them, striding purposefully into the tenement.

He slows his pace to catch his breath again after the arduous walk, the late-afternoon sun still fierce. He advances calmly toward the end of the hallway, accompanied by the stench of the bathrooms by the entrance and the fetid water of a turtle in a washbowl. When he reaches Emilia and Pepe's room, the hair of his neck stands on end.

"What the hell is going on here?" he asks out loud, seeing that the door has been sealed off.

Mafuco

The bets resume on Saturday, May 24, after Migue's trip to Pinar del Río to forage for food and the launch of Chicho's little business making sandals with soles fashioned out of tires and leather stolen from the baseball glove factory. The day's figures are 2088 migrants and 566 boats. Ángel loses when he bets that 1 will come up as the last digit in both categories, convinced that the winning number will be El Number One, El Caballo, El Fifo, Barbatruco, Patilla — ubiquitous on posters, in addresses on radio and TV, in people's comments around the clock and in Ángel's own thoughts.

A few days later, *Granma* roughly explains there was an error in *Noticias de Mariel* on Monday, June 2. When the Tuesday issue was finalized, a discrepancy was found between the number of boats still docked at the port and the figure reported the previous day, taking into consideration how many vessels had left for the US that day.

Each of the three men insists on interpreting the text his own way and the dispute grows more and more heated.

"Gentlemen, let's leave it there for now," Migue suggests. "Let's collect the money as if nothing had happened at all. We're the only ones who even dream of trusting *The Liar*."

They unanimously approve the proposal. Chicho says he'll spend the rest of the night working on his sandals business and Ángel shows Migue how to bet on the license plates of cars passing through the street, like he used to do in Caibarién when he was young. The two friends spend around fifteen minutes on the corner of Infanta and Pedroso, drinking from a bottle of Decano rum until Bienve shows up, takes a few swigs and invites them to smoke a joint in the Parque La Normal.

"Lots of people hope to get rich overnight with this game," Ángel says minutes later, when Bienve asks about the neighborhood legmen. "Others are satisfied with a little nibble once in a while so they don't always turn up among the losers. It's like trying to get a silk purse from a sow's ear but it relaxes me more than a crossword puzzle."

"Silk purse from a sow's ear? Each crazy man to his own," Migue says like a ventriloquist, trying not to laugh and inadvertently exhale the smoke from the joint.

The bottle is empty in no time at all as they pass it from mouth to mouth, thirsty from the marijuana. Bienve then offers to go to Carraguao in search of more weed and Ángel leaves to fetch paper to roll with.

Shortly thereafter, Ángel jogs back down San Joaquín with a piece of the paper bag from his monthly twelve-pound rice ration. He feels like a little boy who doesn't want to go to bed. The pavement slips like a mat underfoot as he runs and jumps from here to there, holding his breath to avoid the stench of the sewers spilling into the intersection with Estévez. Once he reaches Pedroso, he slows to a walk so he won't show up sweaty and with his tongue hanging out.

In the park now, his second toke on the joint makes him nauseous and his frisky spirit shifts into a mixture of defenselessness and paranoia that claws at his insides. Standing in front of his friends, who are sprawled on a stone and iron bench, he glances around in all directions. He's afraid the police will come, but what really makes him shiver is the sight of the place where he was attacked and hit in the face. He has a premonition that dozens of little uniformed warriors, lying in wait behind the benches and among the trees, will besiege him at any moment.

Luckily, Bienve finishes off what's left of the joint and all but jumps to his feet. Migue follows suit and the three set out with no particular destination in mind. They cross San Joaquín, then Infanta, and follow Amenidad to 20 de

Mayo, crossing there to end up on another bench behind the baseball stadium. Here they fight off their drowsiness with a bottle of 90 proof alcohol mixed with water and coffee that Migue buys from El Cojo in the nearby neighborhood of San Martín. The new hooch is called Mafuco. It smells like rotgut and tastes like death but the name makes Ángel laugh. Walfarina, Huesoetigre, Chispaetrén... The countless Havana-born variants of alcohol and water all have suggestive names, but Ángel doesn't think any of them sounds quite as good as Mafuco.

"Ma-fu-co! Hahahahaha..."

Migue and Bienve are infected by Ángel's contagious guffaws. The three men bring their knees to their chests, rock back and forth, and wriggle around like babies on the wooden bench.

"What's so funny, Mafuuuco?"

"Hahahaha. Good old Mafuquín."

"Mafuquín. Bwahahahaha."

"Oooohh oh oh, fuck. Mafucooo..."

"Oh, shit. Too much."

"Hahahahaha..."

Ángel has briefly forgotten all his troubles, but his stomach reminds him of his promise to bring Felo the photos he's received from Emilia.

"Another bottle?" suggests Migue.

Ángel reckons it's about eight p.m. and decides to leave the photos for another day.

The Can

A little after nine p.m., Ángel reaches the apartment where his brother-in-law Perico lives. He's brought the lists of bets collected from the legmen in Carvajal, Agua Dulce and the Pastorita buildings. It's only his second day on the job in this little world of illicit gambling and he's already starting to reap the profits. If things keep going this well, he estimates as he climbs the stairs, he'll be able to buy Obdulio's Chevrolet '53 and start charging passengers for rides. During the day, not at night. And not through all of Havana; just from the bus station directly to Santiago de las Vegas, via Rancho Boyeros Avenue. On the way back, he'll only pick up passengers traveling light, because he'll have the trunk full of food, both for him and for retail. Then the money will be in the bag.

He knocks on the door and almost immediately it slides open a few inches.

"Come in," says a twenty-something man. "Agent Chávez, from the Technical Department of Investigations."

With the swift gestures of an illusionist, the young man flashes then conceals an authority ID as Ángel crosses the threshold. Of the dozen people in the small apartment's living/dining room, three look like plainclothes TDI agents and the rest, Ángel assumes, must be collectors who, like himself, have fallen into the same trap.

"Follow me," he is ordered after being frisked.

They move into the adjacent bedroom.

"Put all your things on the bed."

Given the age difference and the fact that the kid is on duty, despite being in civilian clothes, shouldn't he address him more formally? This is what passes through Ángel's mind as the young man meticulously inspects his wallet and shoes.

"Now your clothes."

When Ángel takes off his pants, the lists, which he'd slipped between the two pieces of the crotch of his athletic underwear, remain perfectly concealed. To keep his expression blank, he shifts his gaze from the window to a vase of artificial flowers placed on top of a sewing machine, then back to the window.

"Underwear too," the agent orders, crouching down.

Ángel rolls the garment into a ball and tosses it, sending it soaring over the inquisitor's head and onto the mattress.

"Turn around against the wardrobe and open your legs."

One, two, three silent seconds.

"Open your butt cheeks with your hands."

More silence.

"Get dressed. We're going back to the living room with the others."

"Can I go to the bathroom for a second if we're done with the search? I'm about to piss myself."

"It's over there. Leave the door open."

Ángel breathes a sigh of relief in the bathroom and focuses on the task of urinating, even though he doesn't need to. Taking advantage of the trickling noise, he slowly tears up the lists and brings a handful of paper scraps to his mouth, but an ill-timed constriction in his throat keeps him from swallowing. He can't take the risk of flushing over and over again until all the pieces of paper disappear down the drain, so he gets rid of them by poking them into the narrow space between the toilet tank and the wall.

*****

Ángel is the last of the detainees to be distributed around different units of the National Revolutionary Police force. Handcuffed and seated between two agents in the back seat of an almost hermetically sealed GAZ van, he can see through the windshield that they're leaving Palatino behind and heading in the direction of Altahabana.

They finally stop in front of the Provincial Police Operations Unit at 100 and Aldabó, where they get him out of the vehicle, remove his handcuffs, and lead him to a kind of reception area that his escorts call "the desk". There, an officer asks for his ID card, wallet, watch, belt, shoelaces, and the contents of his pockets; everything will be stored in a Manila envelope.

"You're 4-5-9-8-2. Learn those five digits by heart, because that's what they'll be calling you from now on," the man tells him, writing the number on the envelope and on a slip of paper he hands to Ángel. "Do you have a relative who can bring you soap, towel, toothbrush and toothpaste?"

"My son, but he's in the Military Service," Ángel responds indifferently.

How long will it take for him to get out of here? He thought they'd ask him a couple of questions and let him go right away. For now, in exchange for his son's full name and what he can remember of the military unit's contact information, the officer hands him a kind of mat and orders him to enter an adjacent compartment, where they take his fingerprints and a mugshot, and conduct a fresh body search. Naked, he has to crouch down, bend over and show his ass again. Then, with his hands behind him, he is frogmarched up a wide staircase. On the first landing, there are padlocked gates and guards armed to the teeth. They proceed into a long hallway that reeks of sweat and despair. Along both sides, every ten feet or so, are barred doors with metal panels, bolts and padlocks.

"Get behind that wall," barks one of the two accompanying guards. "All the way to the back. Don't come out until I tell you to."

From behind the brick partition parallel to the wall, Ángel hears footsteps, the sound of a bolt, a door opening, a metallic slam, and the bolt clattering again.

"You can come out now," he is told.

"Hands behind your back," the second guard reminds him.

As he enters the hallway again, he sees that another guard has been posted in a corner and infers that his role is to direct the traffic of detainees. Then, without a word, he is led into one of the cells on the right.

71

As the door clangs shut behind him with a rusty screech, Ángel remains motionless, sinking into darkness and a humid stench. After a few seconds, as his eyes start adjusting to the poor lighting, he sees a few items of clothing hanging by the entrance, right in front of his face. Underwear. And then he makes out the eyes of a man. Black. About fifty years old, with sharp cheekbones. The only thing he can think to do is take two steps forward, extend his right hand and introduce himself.

"Ángel."

"Paco. First time you've been in the clink? Where would you rather sleep? Top bunk or bottom?"

"Top, if you don't mind."

The man clears one of the two rickety upper beds, consisting of a sort of metal tray suspended by two chains and pivoting around some metal rings built into the wall.

"Relax, anyone can end up here. A manager just as soon as a butcher or a guy who's run someone over," the man adds, taking the mat from under Ángel's arm and laying it out on the bare iron, seven feet long by little more than eighteen inches wide.

"Thanks, brother."

"This little rug is your mattress. Better behave so they don't take it away from you."

Ángel stretches out on his back across the thin layer and tries to stay still — he doesn't want any trouble with the bony Paco. His gaze wanders along the ceiling as his brain tries to make sense of everything that's happening. Hands crossed under his nape, supporting his neck, he moves his head to inspect the cell. It measures ten by seven feet at most, with the first two feet to the left of the door, as you enter, occupied by a hole for a latrine and a water faucet. The cell is about thirteen feet high, entirely closed off, except for a kind of vent, very high up, that seems to form an angle inside the wall to allow light and air to enter while preventing any view of the outside world, even if a man were to hoist himself up on another's shoulders. Apart from the vent, there's a small hatch in the middle of the door, just big enough for a tray and a glass to pass through. Ángel has already seen that the opening has its own tiny door with a bolt on the outside, and hopes to soon confirm that it's used for passing food into the cell.

This Paco fellow proves to be quite communicative. According to the explanations he offers from his own bunk, the water is turned on for fifteen minutes three times a day, and one has to take quick advantage of it if there are more than two occupants. The light is turned on when the guards feel like it, usually at six in the morning and six in the evening. Paco is chatting with him because he's his cellmate, but Ángel won't get the chance to speak with anyone else here, except for the guards, who won't even give him the time of day.

"Another thing: they do a roll call from time to time. They open the hatch, say 'count', and we each have to lean out and say our number."

Ángel wonders who would ever try to escape from this place, what with all the bars and guards.

It's late, maybe around midnight, but he makes use of his cellmate's willingness and, like an apprentice, keeps asking everything he needs to know if he's going to survive. The master offers a few more details, yawns, and says goodnight. And so, without food or a shower, without soap, towel, toilet paper or toothpaste, or even clothes other than what he's got on his back, Ángel tries to settle on his mat.

It takes him half the night to fall asleep.

*****

A furious racket jolts him awake. He's barely slept because of his hunger and teeming thoughts — not to mention the fluorescent tube that, mounted behind a grate and a scrap of acrylic in its own niche above the door, has glared into his face for the past hour.

"What's going on?"

"I don't know, but that's someone kicking on a cell door," Paco responds.

"Open up! This man's gonna burn to death!" they hear someone shout.

The corridor resounds with the clatter of hasty footsteps, angry male voices shouting, the slam of a door and more footsteps. Then silence returns.

Their breakfast — sugared water and a small chunk of stale bread — doesn't take long to arrive. Then the stories begin. Ángel goes first. Afterwards, his companion explains that he's a barber by profession and it seems that someone in the neighborhood reported him for marijuana trafficking. The police showed up at his house, a German Shepherd dog went wild over a pair of scissors, they took them to the lab and proved he'd used them to cut the stuff. Paco alleged that, although he did consume marijuana, he never trafficked it.

*****

They've been getting on so nicely, just the two of them in the cell, and now this new kid has to come along. Ángel is convinced he's some kind of maniac; the only thing he does is scratch his head and his balls. He frets that the guy's got lice. Just two days earlier, Paco had said: "At least we're on our own, 'cause if they stick one of those arrogant kids in with us who doesn't show any respect, well, things could go sour and there's no telling what we'll have to do."

Ángel's reflections are interrupted by a shout through the hatch:

"4-5-9-8-2!"

"Here!"

"Get dressed. I'm coming for you."

Could he have a visitor? Is he free to go? He has no idea where they'll take him, but he obeys at once. The soldier detains him in the tiny space between the metal door and the hall, orders him to put his hands behind his back, explains that he's not going to handcuff him, and, drawing close to Ángel's cheek, whispers:

"Listen closely. We're going to see the case officer. If you confirm to him who the legmen and collectors are, the ones we've got on file anyway, you'll be back on the street in no time. And if you have more information, it'll be kept secret here. But remember what I'm saying to you so you won't regret it later: your case could get more complicated depending on what the others say, and some have already talked quite a bit."

Ángel makes a gesture of acquiescence. He's glad to go off for interrogation and wherever else they send him as long as there's fresh air. He's beyond relaxed: they have no evidence against him.

Then, the same hallway routine is then repeated, including the partition and the echo of footsteps. However, this time they go down the stairs instead of up and, after following corridors this way and that, he ends up sitting in an air-conditioned cubicle before the case officer. The man has laid out some photos across the desk. With no preamble, he starts firing off questions:

"Do you know any of these individuals? Do you know anything about number-running in El Canal or other neighborhoods?"

Some of the faces are familiar to him, but they could easily just be people he's seen out and about, on buses or waiting in queues, over the twenty years he's lived in Cerro.

"I don't know. I may have seen some of them around, but I don't know them. And they don't know me, either. I'm sure of it."

The officer tips his head forward slightly and crosses his arms as if to say "OK, let's start again".

"There's a network that…"

"I don't have anything to do with any network," Ángel protests.

The interrogation goes on for half an hour. The officer remains calm, occasionally shaking his head as if in disbelief before showing Ángel the same photos and asking him the same questions over and over again. Ángel mechanically recites the answers he's been rehearsing day and night. His main worry is that, after the heat in the cell, the powerful air-conditioning could tear into his lungs.

"We want to hear what you know. If what you did was a crime, you'll have to pay for it — but only for your own actions and not for what other people have done," the man insists.

"But, officer, if the police have no proof of who's a legman and who isn't, how would I know? I swear, I've never run numbers or gambled in my whole life. That day, I was just unlucky enough to visit my brother-in-law. There's nothing else happening here. You guys have the means to confirm that. I can't tell you anything else because I can't just invent something I don't know about."

He gives the same answers to the same questions every single day without losing his sanity. He doesn't get the impression that they're trying to browbeat him with what others have said about him, as that soldier kid suggested — maybe he's seen too many American movies. His own film is simply repeated over and over again. The same script, the same dialogues, with a small change in the cast once in a while: the officer. But it is basically the same movie. Every day.

*****

Entering the cell, the blond man makes a gesture as if crossing himself.

"What circle are you from?" Paco asks him.

"Efí Embemoró."

"Me, Otán Efó. Paco, from Regla."

"Felipe, from Colón."

The two men make curious movements with their hands, which Ángel interprets as a ritual greeting. They must be Abakuas from different branches, he thinks, based on what he's learned from Paco about the secret fraternity. With this fourth resident, the place is now full to capacity. Ángel bristles. He's sure he won't be able to sleep tonight, since he has no idea what kind of problems might arise in the tiny cell: perhaps someone will be beaten up or raped, and God knows who that someone might be. To top it all off, his groin starts to prickle.

*****

He's received the unexpected news that he has a visitor, and this time he's led through underground corridors to a room that's far-removed from the cells — so much so that Ángel is convinced he's ended up in a different building altogether. The day is turning out quite well so far: after breakfast, the kid with lice was removed from the cell, and now this wonderful news. Who could have come to visit him if not Eduardito?

And indeed it is: he has fifteen minutes to talk with his son on a couch, in the presence of an officer who watches and listens to everything. Eduardo has brought a nail-clipper, several days' worth of newspapers, a towel, a bar of soap and some clean clothes, and gets straight to the point. He has found out which district attorney is taking care of the case, the only person who can exchange the pre-trial detention for bail so that Ángel can await his sentence in the outside world. Eduardo will go and see him when he's serving the public. He already has a pass arranged for the day in question. While his father uses the nail-clipper, the young man explains that there are so many people involved in this case that no one can get their hands on the file: it could be at the district attorney's office, here, there or anywhere. This is why what could have been a detention of only a few hours has turned into weeks.

After the visit, Ángel is brought back to the desk, where the officers ask him what he's been brought. They open and shake out the towel and clothes, warn him that he can't keep anything to read or write on, prod the soap twice in different places with a nail driven through a plank, and send him back to his cell.

Paco and Felipe are still there, playing checkers on a grid they've scratched across one of the lower metal pallets. For chips they use cigarette filters, some crumpled, others not. After exchanging a few words about the visit, Ángel entertains himself by feeling and caressing the clothes he's been brought. One of the garments is a shirt of Eduardo's that still carries his smell. Ángel won't put it on; he'll keep it folded neatly so that he can smell it when bitter melancholy fills his throat.

As the Abakuas focus on their game, Ángel wonders what will happen to him. Gone are those fantasies about how to spend the money he was yet to make. The story of the milkmaid and her pail — it never ends well. I should know that by now, he scolds himself, embittered by a bad moment in a distant past. How many weeks has he been in the can? Three? He's starting to lose all sense of time, which is devouring him like a mute old man from within the shadows and tedium. He has no way of distinguishing a Monday from a Saturday. Either one feels like an eternity. These are dog days, ageing him and weighing on his ribs. A single day in the can drags on as long as five or seven outside, give or take. What's happening out there as he remains stuck in here? Life beyond 100 and Aldabó resembles his own funeral — unattended by his friends. Only Eduardito has come to console and help him. His son. His blood.

And, once again, back to the wheel of thought and blame, to the seconds in their unflinching and relentless — but excruciatingly slow — movement forward.

*****

A new day begins with the number he won't forget for many years.

"4-5-9-8-2!"

"Here."

"Get dressed and get all your things together. You're leaving."

He's leaving? He's going home? Or to Valle Grande, the prison for unsentenced detainees, where he could rot away? He collects his few belongings and bids a hasty farewell to his cellmates. Their moderation and respect have earned his affection. Especially Paco; Ángel would have gone crazy without his conversation.

Around eight in the morning, waiting on a bench next to the room where they are keeping his possessions, his number is called one more time.

"You're on probation, pending trial. When they give you a date, show up with the proof of bail the bank has granted and they'll return your money. If you end up in a police unit again for any reason at all, and it emerges that you've been released on bail, you'll be back in pre-trial detention. So, to stay out of trouble, I suggest you don't go anywhere with big groups of people. You can't leave the province. If we need to ask you something as part of the investigation, we'll call you and you have to be available. Understood?"

"Understood."

He's given his things and taken to the front door of the building.

"Follow that path and you'll see the street," a last guard tells him, gesturing toward a fence.

Ángel obeys, asking no questions, and heads off down the fenced-in passageway bordering an area for cars. He touches his several-day-old beard and tries to convince himself that the month he's spent in the enormous bunker behind him has been nothing more than a nightmare. After walking fifty or so yards, he still can't see the exit and quickens his step.

"Papi!" shouts someone from the other side of the fence.

"Oh, kiddo!"

*****

Ángel was the only person in the case without a criminal background and against whom there was no evidence at all. He was a key production worker and the family unit's chief breadwinner. After listening to Eduardo's arguments, the district attorney granted the change of measure that same week. The boy paid two thousand pesos in bail that he'd managed to raise among some of his friends and Migue.

It was time for Ángel to find out how things had ended up in El Canal. And so, as soon as he left 100 and Aldabó, he made his way there — without his son — instead of going home. But all he could get out of his sister-in-law, other than the fact that Perico was locked up and incommunicado, was: "I heard someone knocking on the door and, when I looked out the window, I saw it was some suspicious-looking guy, so I ran and put the lists into the pressure cooker."

Once again, on the street, he detects the same indecipherable smell he'd noticed inside the apartment. Is it the goddamn neighborhood, something he's brought with him from prison, or is it the stench of his own fate? No one had to tell him he would remain under police surveillance. The police would surely know about his detention by now; and the committee, the union, the party members in the workshop — where they may no longer be expecting him. It could also be the stink of betrayal. This time Perico will end up under lock and key, or he's a police informer, the fucker. No one's going to Ángel Ribot with tall tales about pressure cookers, let alone to the dozen in the can! If Perico is released, he'd better disappear from Havana and all of Cuba, too, because they'll chase him wherever he goes. Of course, people could think the same about him: that he's a rat, an informer — after all, as soon as he was inside the network, several of its key pieces went through the roof. But he's unconcerned about what a handful of leeches and gamblers might think of him. Won't a whole lot of other people brand him as antisocial scum no matter what? In any case, as he crosses the Canal neighborhood under the stare of fierce people in tenement doorways and on every corner, his chest pounds with the excitement of feeling himself anchored in the very foundation of social interaction on the island: suspicion. I suspect you're part of the system, you suspect the same of me, we all suspect the same of everyone else, and life continues along its course of containment and restraint, exactly as the powers that be want it.

Bearing his new stigma, he instinctively opens and tenses his hands as he lengthens the movements of his arms accompanying every step. If he wanted, he could sing aloud:

Don't you mess with me
'Cause I'm a fire-eater

Route 61

When the driver sees that, at the Esquina de Tejas stop, more passengers intend to get on than will probably get off, he decides to halt the bus dozens of yards beyond the stop, so that the ones who want to get off can do so and no one else will board. Unfortunately, almost everyone already knows the trick, so lots of people have gathered around alternative stopping places. Others dash forward and cling like suction cups to the right side of the moving vehicle.

These vicissitudes are part of the everyday adventure implicit in traveling from one end of Havana to the other, and it's public knowledge that the Yankee embargo is at fault, Eduardo says to himself, hanging partway out of the bus as he watches the high gateways of the old villas zoom past along Calzada del Cerro. Behind them are Monte's two miles of neoclassical colonnades and blackened façades.

The bus stops at the corner of Cruz del Padre for the Latinoamericano Stadium. The passengers who haven't been able to reach the fare box at the front have to get off and make room for more. Colliding with Eduardo's legs, a German Shepherd puppy tries to follow an almond-eyed, thirty-something woman out through the front door, but is met with resistance at the other end of the leash. What a shock! As if keeping an eye open for prevention patrols weren't enough; and officers, too, just in case. Eduardo is well aware that, if they nab him on the run, he could get twenty-four hours in the can plus seventy-two more of service. His head is clean shaven and he's wearing his olive-green recruit uniform, which is why he doesn't want to cross half of Havana hanging out of a bus or descend to the sidewalk at every stop.

Precisely to avoid hanging out the side, he'd waited over an hour at the start of the route, seated on the old Teatro Martí's stone wall, his back against the iron fence, twisting his neck to watch the street cats in the abandoned building. Unfortunately, when he decided to buy something to eat from the stand in front of the Payret movie theater about a hundred yards from the stop, and started walking, glancing behind him every once in a while in case the bus approached, it did, and he had to head back in a rush, only to end up among the last to board.

Which is why, now, instead of waiting patiently on the sidewalk for everyone who wants to get off, he decides to reboard through the double-width middle door. But the bus lurches into motion and he has to turn around, break into a run, grab one of the folding doors with his left hand, clutch at the gasket of the adjacent window with his right, and jump in order to get a foothold. He's instantly pushed inside by two men who are trying to do more or less the same thing behind him. He remains motionless on the edge of the upper step, planted there on the tips of his toes — but at least he's no longer the last one hanging out of the door.

He's picturing the parade of cast iron swans and snakes at the Bocoy Rum Factory on the left when he hears the driver argue with someone. The bus comes to a sudden halt and the passengers suffer the jolt of the emergency brake as they pass the curve of the Santovenia Retirement Home. For a moment Eduardo thinks there's going to be trouble, but the driver simply announces that he's combining the Covadonga and Jurídico stops. Then, he opens the three doors and shouts:

"Felicia, get off here to buy bread!"

"I'm gonna lose my seat."

The driver shakes his head, pulls a red handkerchief from his pants pocket, and leaps out into the street with surprising agility.

"My God, it's hot!"

"It's like an oven in here. Where's the driver disappeared to?"

Inside the vehicle, the heat and humidity seem to rise by the second. Eduardo consoles himself by thinking that he'll soon be free of his horrible uniform. Until recently, he hadn't had any idea what he would do after his military service. He'd always wanted to go to college like his sister, but he couldn't imagine it would ever be possible: he had ended up outside the educational system altogether, and when he finished his time in the draft, he'd be as old as many students were when they got their degrees. The solution had fallen on him like manna from heaven in the form of a ruling from the Secretary of the Armed Revolutionary Forces: the so-called Order 18, which would soon open the doors of higher education to young people with pre-university studies who had completed military service.

His thoughts and gaze have become lost among digressions, projects and sweaty necks. Then a sudden thud of something heavy falling to the floor brings his eyes to a head of braided black hair, a woman's clear forehead and a hand picking up a hardcover book. When the young woman straightens up, he also sees two shy green eyes.

Eduardo returns to his ruminations on the past, on things that might have been. He would have liked to study Classics or Art History. He ruled out Journalism as soon as the possibility arose because access to all information was already restricted enough; he wouldn't want to deal with daily government censorship if he had to act as a spokesperson someday. He refused to be yet another conducting wire in the closed circuit of official propaganda. Anyway, even though he had the academic record required for the other two majors, he was excluded from the integral ranking for university access at a meeting in which his classmates followed to their convenience the slogan *du jour*: "The university is for revolutionaries".

Heavy-eyed in the lethargy of midday, he recalls how he's reached where he is now. It's a relief to avoid the present, even if his thoughts do not lead him to a probable college life, but rather to a past as oppressive as the present day. Which "school-goes-to-the-countryside" was it that he'd been expelled from? Was it in tenth or eleventh grade?

His first act of transgression was putting on a mini rock concert during the "Recreation" activity. With brooms for guitars, manes made of towels, and a drum set improvised from a wooden suitcase and an aluminum cup, he and three guys from his brigade played "Inside Looking Out". In response to the applause and calls for an encore from four rocker cats, they continued with "Satisfaction". Neither of the two acts had been scheduled, and punishment came swiftly: cleaning the latrines for a whole week after the regular workday in the banana fields.

The second, more serious misdeed supposedly involved forbidden gambling and wrongful use of medication. In reality, it was just that Nora Ferro, the fearsome Spanish teacher, had caught him in the dorm during the workday, playing cards with Wicho while Sergito shouted "Solid fuel!" and tossed onto a bunk bed the aspirins he'd been given in the infirmary for a feigned migraine. The disciplinary court — composed of Caridad, the camp director; Benigno "the Chemist"; and Salvador, the Marxism teacher and secretary of the Party's base committee, along with representatives from the Union of Communist Youth and the Student Federation of Secondary Education — decided to expel them.

Aside from the harsh voices and contemptuous glances of his accusers, another series of images plays back in his memory: the journey in Salvador's car along the dirt road and, when they reached the interprovincial bus station, being ordered to get out and never return to camp. He felt like an abandoned dog.

These incidents stood out a few years later, during that delightful meeting when the students evaluated each other in order to create an integral hierarchy for accessing university majors. Eduardo couldn't go because he was in bed, with a fever and acute diarrhea. Two days later, he found out about the condemnatory terms issued by the young woman who had represented the Union of

Communist Youth in the countryside disciplinary court. As he was told, Katiuska asserted that both he and his "accomplices" had gotten off easy after their expulsion because she had personally intervened so that the episode wouldn't appear on their records, and the initial charge of "drug abuse" would be reduced to a euphemistic "wrongful use of medication". But the whole school was already tired of so much indiscipline and immaturity, not to mention ideological diversionism. To make matters worse, Katiuska opportunely reminded those present, Eduardo Ribot hadn't even deigned to attend such an important meeting, which only proved his apathy and contempt for higher education.

He's roasting in his uniform shirt, now soaked in sweat, and he can't see the female student amid the forest of arms. But he does see a clearing toward the back. In the hope of finding a seat, he makes his way through the immobilized passengers until he reaches an empty spot near a middle-aged man, barefoot, speaking either to the book he's leafing through or to the faces he's making — it's hard to tell which. The bus lurches into motion and Eduardo nearly falls onto the man. Standing beside him, Eduardo tries to read along: "the energy of an ideal fluid, with neither viscosity nor friction, in circulating through a closed conduit, remains constant along the fluid's journey". When he senses the intrusion, the unhinged man flips rapidly through the pages, leaving Eduardo with no choice but to stop reading and gaze out of the window. It smells like it might rain despite the brilliant sun hanging high in the sky.

"Driver, here's the stop!" a woman shouts as the bus makes a long turn at top speed around the curve of the pizzeria and the movie theater.

"This is the 61, madam. It doesn't stop at Maravillas," explains an old man with a refined manner.

"Where will it take me, then?"

"Católicas Cubanas, if indeed he wishes to stop."

The bus passes the next stop without slowing. Amid the shouts, a drunk babbles and unwittingly steps on several passengers' feet. Muttering and laughter spring up around him.

"Show some respect and you'll be respected," the man's voice rises. "I was a member of the Suicide Platoon of the Eighth Column. With El Vaquerito. A little respect, okay, huh? 'Cause nobody knows who's who around here, where anyone comes from or where anyone's going. And watch out for those pickpockets. They're collectin', if you get me."

Checking their handbags and pockets, the passengers distance themselves from the old Rebel Army combatant as much as they can.

"Listen up," the driver says. "Get off here for Cerro and Boyeros. There'll be no alighting at the stop or the traffic light or anywhere after that. The next one's at 26, so keep that in mind."

Eduardo follows the driver's advice, taking advantage of the human tide to keep moving toward the back. It's 12:30 on the only wristwatch he can spot and he has an overwhelming urge to take off his uniform. He should be getting off here, but they haven't even reached the intersection of Calzada del Cerro and Primelles. He'll get off at 26 instead and switch in Ciudad Deportiva. Lifting his head to breathe more easily, he rediscovers the young student's gaze as she approaches the back of the bus. He calculates that, instead of catching another bus to Fontanar at Ciudad Deportiva, and then the 50 through El Chico and El Wajay to El Cano, he could stay on this one till it reaches Mariano, where he can catch the 50. It's riskier, though, because at Mariano there will be preventive police patrols and red berets searching for escaped recruits. But he needs those green eyes.

The driver has brought the bus to a standstill, leaving its engine running, in order to get off and knock at the door of a house. When no one answers, he jumps over the sidewall of the entrance hall into an abandoned lot almost totally covered in debris. There, he grabs a baseball bat from a little boy playing ball with a buddy and asks the latter for a toss, quick.

"Just one, c'mon, the bus is stopped outside. Stop being a pain."

"Strike!" calls the boy who's been forced to serve as the catcher.

"Another one, but throw it good. Come through the middle."

"Strike two."

"One more and that's all. One more and I'll go, I mean it."

"Strike! You're out! Okay, that's it."

"Last one. But make it a good one, dammit."

"You're out! Stop being a pain and give me the bat," the catcher begs. "Get out of here, man! Mo-o-ommm!"

While the idling bus hums on the roadside, the mother emerges with a coffee for the driver, the boy picks up his bat, and the game is resumed.

"Don't you know you can't smoke on the bus?" a man in a long-sleeved, paint-spattered gray shirt reprimands a teenager.

"Who says?"

"Who? I do, kid. Give it here."

Within seconds, the man pulls the lit cigarette from the boy's mouth and tosses it through the window, just as the bus starts moving.

"So you're gonna get off at the next stop and snatch the next one I light up, right?" the boy taunts, pulling a squashed pack of cigarettes from his back pocket.

"If you light it, I'm the one who's gonna make you swallow it," another man speaks up, this time a burly forty-something mulatto.

The boy is with three mates who have spent much of the ride hanging out of the windows or getting on and off through them. Thanks to the repositioning of passengers anxious about a tumultuous brawl breaking out, Eduardo finds himself facing the perfectly sculpted nose and chin of the student, who supports herself with a hand against his chest as she clutches her books with the other.

"Move back a little if you can — there's going to be trouble here," she urges him, her tone somewhere between scared and desperate.

Eduardo shifts backward but, just as swiftly as they ended up pressed together, they each find themselves hemmed in by the plump body of an older woman.

"26 and 51! What the hell's going on back there?" the driver hollers. He stops the bus and opens the doors right in front of the train tracks.

The boys get off in a flash and hurry away, spitting insults.

"Keep going, keep going. The problem was just some sassy kids and I got 'em off," the mulatto explains.

"And I'll make sure they don't get on again," declares the drunk.

"Wait! I'm getting off here," says a woman with an enormous handbag.

As soon as the bus revs up again, Eduardo feels someone touching his right arm. Craning his neck toward the end of the bus, he finds out it's all about a few coins: a passenger who has boarded at the back is trying to pass their fare up to the front. He lifts his right arm, takes the money, reaches out and touches the female student's shoulder, after pausing for a moment to observe her shiny black hair and white neck beneath. Just then, an abrupt turn makes him lose his balance. Luckily, the other bodies keep him upright and he's able to give the coins to another passenger. After the bend, he leans over just enough to move his head past the bulky lady beside him, who gives off an acrid scent of milk of magnesia mixed with alcohol. Eduardo waits in that position, convinced he'll see the girl in a couple of seconds because she'll be looking for him from behind — but she doesn't reappear. In an attempt to make this error into a game, he starts to move his head alternately backward and forward, with a resulting motion of his buttocks like a weightless pendulum, right when the bus enters the hairpin bend at the Puentes Grandes gas station.

"Hold tight — there are elderly people and kids here, and even they are managing to hang on."

A sudden downpour begins. Water is everywhere, as if it were raining more inside the bus than out. Trying to dodge it, passengers collide. Two women yell as they move around and a young man hangs onto the bar of a roof hatch, struggling to pull it shut. When the bus comes to a halt, two leaks of cold water converge in a stream that hits Eduardo in the neck, making him jump just as he notices the girl is getting off. He pushes his way forward through the sea of bodies, leaps out, stumbles through the closing door and almost dashes his brains out on a step that is inexplicably elevated almost three feet above the sidewalk.

Most of the people who have left the bus run uphill, along a street that forms a sharp angle with the main road. Others cross the street to wait in a food-allocation store. Eduardo can't see the girl anywhere, but he spots that the dairy store where he has sought shelter is selling soft cheese without demanding to see ration books. He buys four pieces and immediately gobbles down two, leaving the wrappers on some piled-up pine and bagasse boxes.

Beneath the lintel, as he stares out into the rain and wipes his mouth with the handkerchief that Ángel gave him as a birthday present, he decides to cross the street to the store to see if he can find some bread.

After climbing some steps as high as walls and as long as grandstands, he discovers that the ration store is closed and the people huddled in the doorway are squeezed together just the same as in the dairy store and on the bus. But at least he can breathe fresh air here. An overstatement, as, together with the rain, the foul-smelling water of an overflowing sewer pours downhill toward the main road.

"Excuse me," a female voice says next to him just as he clicks his tongue in disgust. "Do you have anything I can clean my hand with?"

Looking up, he finds the student's oval face before him. Her hand appears to be stained with grease.

"Of course," he answers, attentive, as he tucks the remaining cheese into a shirt pocket and pulls out his handkerchief again.

"Oh, but it's so clean I'll feel terrible making it dirty," she says, making a sweet face.

"Don't worry — that's what it's for. Here..."

Eduardo takes the girl's hand.

"Hmm!" he adds, beginning to rub it with the cloth.

"Why do you say 'Hmm'?"

"No reason. Just things that cross my mind. Hey, what's your name?"

"Beatriz. And yours?"

"Eduardo."

"Okay, Eduardo, so why did you say 'Hmm'?"

He improvises.

"You know what? It's a good thing this has happened. What I mean is, because your hand's dirty, we can look at the length and breadth of the lines on your palm. See this one here, for example?"

Beatriz smiles.

"I don't believe in that stuff but I see the line. And? What's so special about that one in particular?"

"You can rest assured it's nothing bad."

"You've got me intrigued. Do you really know how to read palms?"

"Why would that surprise you? There's education for all, but this country only has a handful of half-literate palmists. It's a disgrace. Believe me, there aren't many of us who actually know what we're doing, if you'll forgive my saying so."

"Very funny." The girl now gestures toward La Tropical beer factory and El Bosque de la Habana forest. "Are you in the military unit over that way?"

"I wish. Mine's in El Cano, an hour from here by bus. I came to see a friend in La Ceiba, but I decided to get off early to escape that hellish bus and buy some food. I'm not in a rush and it's still raining, so, if you want, I'll tell you what I can see. It's pretty interesting, I have to say."

"Well, since you say that everything you've seen is good, I'm curious now. If you see something bad, don't tell me — I don't wanna know.

Beatriz offers her hand.

"Let's see. Let me clean you off a bit more."

The girl bursts into easy laughter and brings her free hand to her mouth.

"You're tickling me!"

"Take a deep breath and deal with it. Ready?"

"Ready," she says, her eyes shut.

She lightly squeezes his forearm. Swept along by the new physical contact that appears to have dissolved all previous distrust, Eduardo slips the cloth over her skin in a near caress.

"And now?" the arch of her fine brows seems to inquire over her intense stare.

He wants to cover her beautiful face with kisses. Instead, he says:

"I'm not displeased at all by what I see, actually. Your lifeline is long and deep. It doesn't say how long you'll live, just your health and vitality, you know? And now I expect you'd like to know what your heart line says."

The girl nods with a smile and he loosens the reins of his imagination. His words trigger the same attractive smile, which makes him tremble slightly.

"Now you're just teasing me."

"I'm telling you what I see. No more, no less. I may be wrong, but it's your fault if so: I can't concentrate if you're laughing. I'll also confess that I'm so hungry I can't even see straight. Forgive me for changing the subject to something so mundane. I don't want to bore you."

"You're not boring me at all. In fact, I think you've earned yourself a glass of malt and an empanada pasty."

"And where's that? You're the one who's teasing now. I haven't had malt for years."

"There's a place just around the corner. If they don't have any, I have some at home — I only bought it yesterday. In any case, it's stopped raining and there's no reason for us to be here. I don't know about you, but I have a million things to do, starting with an assignment for school that's gotten me on the verge of despair."

Eduardo remembers he needs to get back to the unit, but he still has time to spare. The later and darker it gets, the better.

"What are you studying?"

"Economics. I don't know why I haven't paid anyone to type up my work."

"If you want, I could loan you my typewriter. I'm not using it at the moment because, as you can see, I'm in uniform."

"You seriously have a typewriter? So you must also know how to type. A one-man band!"

*****

The little girl in the photo beneath the glass top on the bedside table smiles for the camera. She glows with the candor of innocence and her smile reveals a hint of the mischievousness in the look she gives Eduardo, ten years later, in the mirror over the dresser, smoothing her hair, a bone hair slide between her teeth.

The room smells of ozone and bodily fluids — also tobacco, malt and empanadas. Still drenched in sweat and exhausted by ecstasy, Eduardo delights his eyes on the roundness of Beatriz's buttocks, the curve of her waist, the ample breasts that aren't yet insinuated in the photo. They drove him wild a few minutes ago and they'll drive him wild again in no time at all. For now, with his head resting on the pillow and a smile on his lips, he remembers a friend saying "It's easy to come and hard to get away". He doesn't agree: he could stay in this room with Beatriz until the end of time.

The tinkling of the rain against the window's zinc sheet is the perfect soundtrack for brushing against the girl's smooth skin. She has just stretched out at his side to kiss him. Feeling the sweetness of her lips, Eduardo can't imagine any better manifestation of paradise. And he brushes away the thought of his return to the hellish military unit.

Gilbert and King

"I don't think I've told you this before, Isa, but it's important for you to know. My mom gave birth to me in the Caibarién house, in the room where my old man kept food, tools and all sorts of other shit. I was a twin, but my sibling was born strange - with a huge head and crab claws, they say. From what I've heard, it was the first to come out. It started scrabbling across the floor and vanished somewhere into the pigpens we kept out behind the ditch and the guava trees."

Isabel is unfazed by the story her husband continues to relate.

"My old man scared it off by throwing stones at it every day, but it kept coming back when we fed the dogs. One time they almost killed it. Boys my age used to taunt me with the story, but then I busted Barreto's eyebrow and two teeth, and no little fucker ever said another word after that."

The woman doesn't get up and go into the kitchen to prepare the coffee steeping in its muslin bag. Nor does she lift her breast with her forearm, the mannerism that so irritates Felo. She simply stares at him, motionless, not saying a word. Would it be worthwhile, really, giving her more details about how the two of them tangled themselves up in the clothesline and fell to the ground together? And how by lashing out with the machete this way and that, he managed to get it into the ditch? It continued to drag itself along, the bastard, until he finished it off with the tip of the ox-goad leaning against one of the pens.

When the alarm goes off on the bedside table, Felo tries to open his eyes, but they immediately smart from the light filtering in through the window. He turns over in bed, one eye half open now, and switches off the alarm. He's amazed that it's already six in the morning and remembers that today, Tuesday, September 14, 1988, is going to be a long day.

*****

Felo sees a truck coming down the road. It's not Gonzalo's. He walks from one side to the other without straying far from the corner. He has all the documents needed for sorting out the issue of lunch for the brigade. Yesterday he'd had a few too many drinks and today even his soul hurts. He can't keep this up anymore, especially during the week. He remembers that there are several fiber cement sheets still to be laid at the barracks people these days call "modules". Crushed stone is supposed to arrive today. He could take advantage of the volunteers to pour the concrete roof for what will soon be the washrooms, and also lay the foundations for the new intensive care room. The wooden boards have finally arrived, which will save them from having to plaster the ceiling, but their supply problems are ongoing: they still need cables, electrical boards, tiles... Now it turns out that the company can't send any cement workers, the excuse being as ridiculous as the one recently given to him by the albino girl in a pizzeria to avoid serving him a beer: the bottles were divided among the clerks and anyone finishing their own couldn't sell someone else's. At this point, even as brigade chief, he still doesn't know whether they'll go for aluminum or wood carpentry — not that he could care less. But, of course, the Municipal Party people will still come and pester them today, no matter what!

Another truck. Still not the one.

The weekend has flown by, he didn't get around to installing the new sink at home or the windows he's been meaning to put in for quite a while, and the goddamn hurricane is on its way. It's torn through Jamaica and Grand Cayman, and is now heading for the southern coast of Cuba.

Here it comes at last.

"Morning, boss," Lázaro greets him from the right side of the cab.

"How's it going?" Gonzalo asks at the wheel.

"Well, here I am," he responds briskly before hoisting himself up into the back of the truck and rapping his knuckles on the cab roof. "Let's go!"

He grips the cold, rusty iron. Severe weather persists and the streets are deserted. He's already heard the weather forecast: conditions will continue to deteriorate as Gilbert approaches the island.

Passing a pile of junk and debris on Reina and Rayo, the fibroid flashes into Felo's memory, followed by the bag for steeping coffee and Isabel, the person he loves most in the whole world, who treats him so patiently even in his most unsettling dreams. Then he realizes that he forgot to go to the blood bank yesterday, when he could have left early because they'd run out of sand. He can't give blood today because of the alcohol he drank last night. Besides, he won't have time. It'll have to be tomorrow, first thing in the morning, before he goes to the Municipality, he tells himself. After all, there's no way he can ask anyone from the brigade to go to the blood bank for him, given the personal nature of the matter. Why did Eduardo wait so long to tell him? Poor girl. Does her father know she's pregnant and thinking about getting an abortion?

With so many potholes, his memories and worries are bounced away as soon as they emerge. Felo thinks of all the things he has to do and presses them between his temples to protect them from bumps and turns along the road. Tonight, without fail, he'll put in the sink. Over the weekend, the living room window. He can see that several trees in the Parque de la Fraternidad have lost large limbs, and that their foliage, or what little's left of it, trembles horizontally in the wind. Noticing that a traffic sign has ended up on someone's porch, he worries that this coming hurricane Gilbert will be like King, which ravaged the island's central region in 1950. He doesn't remember where it blew ashore, but he endured it personally in Caibarién, where huts were destroyed by the wind, even the sturdiest houses lost their roofs, and bloated dead chickens and pigs were swept away by the current of the Guaní River. In fact, both the Guaní and Bartolomé swelled beyond their banks and morphed into lakes, flooding everything. He hasn't forgotten how the gusts of wind and relentless rain lashed his house while his family stayed awake entire nights of deceptive calm in the face of what could happen.

One of those hurricane days, around six in the morning, his father made him and Angelito go out and bring back a pair of oxen he kept at the foot of Loma de Guajabana hill. The oxen were nowhere to be found and, while the two of them struggled to descend the hundred-odd yards, the air became a visible force, full of solid particles and a noise that took their breath away. The winds must have blown at about a hundred miles an hour. Pulling his younger brother down with him, Felo threw himself to the ground, where they stayed among the protruding roots of a ceiba tree for what seemed like forever. It had been both an exciting and terrible experience.

King reduced his family's crops to a swamp and left the house flooded for several days. He remembers them well because he stayed at his godmother's house in the center of town, and at the end of the week his father abandoned them, fleeing with a neighbor's daughter who lived in a shack on the other side of the train tracks. He doesn't hate him for it. In fact, he's glad his father left them then instead of years later. The shouts, blows and fears all disappeared along with him. Thanks to his absence, Felo and his mother were able to forge a closeness that provided them both with security, comfort and mutual support over time. Felo doesn't think of him on Father's Day — he thinks of her.

The truck leans into a sharp bend around the narrow, muddy space between one pile of blocks and another of steel rods, before halting in front of Agustín, deaf Ibáñez, and Cuco, who are sitting on some wooden planks while they wait.

"Morning. Did you make it back all right yesterday?"

"Yeah, just fine, although I sure had a few drinks. The only thing was that I got stuck in the downpour. Where's everybody?"

"Dunno."

"So how was yesterday? You were tanked!" yells the deaf man, whose sixtieth birthday they were celebrating the day before.

Instead of responding, Felo turns his attention to a young man who is approaching, dragging a shovel behind him.

"Fuck, Iván, how many times do I have to tell you to take care of your tools? Imagine you're fighting a war and that's your gun!"

He knows he doesn't gain anything by being so strict, but he can't behave any other way. What's more, if he weren't the way he is, his bosses wouldn't trust him and his subordinates would walk all over him. Especially the young guys, Che's so-called "new men", with their insolent laziness, and the violent and arrogant way they talk, walk, spit, laugh and completely vanish from their posts every so often.

A few men inside the guard's booth, trying to listen to Radio Reloj, tell him to quiet down. Felo joins them and overhears that the Hurricane of the Century is located at 19.9° north latitude and 85.3° west longitude: 293 miles from Havana. It has intensified overnight and reached category 5, with a wind speed of 180 miles an hour. It's moving northwest, toward the capital.

*****

Not far from the guard station, Eduardo jumps off the footrest of a moving forklift and sits down on the planks with the others. His unusual presence on the construction site at eight in the morning is partly the result of his need to put in hours of "volunteering" in public works. It turns out that the university started by requiring forty hours, then eighty, and now a hundred and twenty. He's tried to do some of them in his uncle's brigade, in the hope that he'll get a certificate for more hours than he actually intends to invest, but the document has yet to materialize.

He remembers the admiration he felt as a little boy for his only uncle, who imbued him with boundless masculinity whenever they saw each other. He can't explain why this childhood fondness has been replaced by a visceral aversion to the intolerant hairy-eared brigade leader, the diehard communist who reproduces the latest flagrant clichés in ridiculous poses. Eduardo's imagination sketches his uncle reciting a hateful prayer every morning, holding the end of his shaving brush in one hand, on the verge of crushing a testicle against the sink. Does he drink vinegar with breakfast? What's with his sour nature, his hostility toward absolutely everyone?

But it's best to hide his antipathy, keep it in, pretend it doesn't exist. More important than the number of volunteer hours he could register with the university is that his uncle finally get hold of the document verifying the donation he's promised for Beatriz's abortion. When he told the staff at the blood bank that he'd just recovered from a bout of flu with a high fever and that he'd taken medication, they told him he wouldn't be allowed to donate for the next two weeks. That's why he needs Felo's blood. Beatriz needs it to get out of this mess. They need the zealot's blood.

To the Smell of Sardines

Eduardo wonders what kind of meaning there can possibly be in his everyday life since he broke up with Beatriz.

This afternoon, he went with Nano and Orejita to the double-bill baseball game in the Latinoamericano Stadium and was thoroughly bored. The only exciting moments involved the umpire's debatable decision to call a foul on a grounder that skirted third base and the out achieved by the Industriales pitcher when he caught a liner headed right for his face.

Without even waiting for the first game to be over, his two friends shook hands and left the stadium — one to go and rest, the other to meet a girl in Lawton.

"I'm gonna stay a little longer to see if this picks up," Eduardo mumbled.

But before five minutes had elapsed, he too left the stadium to flee Beatriz's ghost, which insistently appeared before him in the stands and the lights on the diamond.

He wanders up Consejero Arango, first uphill, then down, and turns left at the end of the street. He is struck by an aseptic odor that envelops him in the whole sorry affair of the pregnancy termination. It is very similar to the smell of the OB/GYN hospital where they got one of the twenty appointments allotted per day for abortions. Both Eduardo and Beatriz had thought that this would be the best solution to the nightmare they were facing. They were wrong.

In vain, he now advances into the streets of the Atarés neighborhood, hoping to run into a friend to kill time with. No one materializes. But his thoughts keep filling with her warm smile. He brings his hands to his face and tells himself: you'll forget her, you'll see.

Downcast, his feet kicking up dust, he reaches the tenement room. He lifts the half net curtain hanging from the doorframe and there's his father, facing away, whistling as he cooks. He moves his head to the beat of an old tune about the criollo night, a beautiful black woman and a bohemian soul.

"Like a cat to the smell of sardines," Ángel says without a glance, bustling about with the pressure cooker, ladle, aluminum pot, skimmer and two plates. "Don't even think about going out again. Food's ready."

Bombs

Pepe gently turns a bottle of Chilean wine by its base as he draws it away from the second glass he's filling. Emilia feels a mix of envy and scorn as she watches how her husband gives his glass a few circular motions in the air before sniffing the swirled wine. He seems to assess the color and delicate cascades that bathe the inner wall of the glass, then fills his mouth and purses his lips as if he were about to whistle. He makes the liquid gurgle.

Emilia watches him discreetly while she readies herself for the inevitable game of associations and evocations. Maybe today it'll be raspberry, cherry, strawberry, walnut, cinnamon, sage, roses, pepper, honey, chocolate, pine or leather. Certainly not dried grass or tar. And what kinds of adjectives will we have for accompaniment? Perhaps creamy, velvety, meaty, greasy, vigorous, fresh, toasted, silky, brilliant, joyful, or perfumed. With a hint of asphalt?

Oh, the connoisseur has lifted his glass. She'd better pay attention now. What could the verdict possibly be?

"To democracy!"

Unnerved, Emilia lifts her glass.

"Do you realize, my love, that in the ten or so years we've been here, we've made this gesture more times than in all the years we lived in Cuba?" he asks without returning his glass to the table.

How could she forget?

"Another toast to this country and how lucky we are that it's taken us in," Pepe repeats.

Emilia lifts her glass, takes a long sip, and listens to him as he goes on about visiting relatives in New York. It's not that she's not keen on the visit, but her husband seems much more enthusiastic about the "Cubafest" than about Central Park, Grand Central Station or the boat trips she wants to go on — not to mention the Immigration Museum. It's true that Pepe's relatives were the ones who got them out of Opa-locka Airport like someone recovering a suitcase in the lost-and-found, but that was a long time ago.

The bell rings and Pepe hurries to open the door. As far as Emilia knows, they're not expecting anyone. When the door closes, however, she hears Abelito, a childhood friend of Pepe's who lives near the Everglades and occasionally comes to Miami — to visit friends and family, he says, but she knows about his shady dealings.

As soon as he steps inside and greets her at a distance, the visitor walks into the kitchen behind his friend, who asks him point-blank: "Did you come up with anything? I'm strapped."

"Brother, what I've got for you here is a high-performance hydroponic bomb," Abel responds, placing a small see-through nylon bag on top of the washing machine. "It costs almost twice what it usually does, but you just try it and tell me it's not worth it."

"And how did you get your hands on it, huh?"

"Ah! It's a long story, so start rolling yourself a doobie while I tell you the short version. Here's some paper. A pal from El Cotorro gave it to me. The guy only just got here. He lives in one of those houses where illegals grow grass and take care of it as if it were theirs in exchange for housing and protection from Immigration."

"Shall I light it up?"

"No point in hanging around! Let me tell you something, bro. This guy's a chemical engineer and accepted this little business 'cause it earns him more than the shit jobs he gets offered. And because he needs a lot of money as soon as possible so he can get his daughter out of Cuba. But he could get a good job any second and screw our supply. I mean, the guy's a scientist. A sci-en-tist and he's selling marijuana. It's crazy! Well, what do you think of the stuff?"

*****

Emilia has brought her wine glass upstairs to the study and feels like writing to Cuba. She searches for words of encouragement, of hope. All that comes to her mind is the distrust directed toward the Marielitos, who in 1980 were arriving around the clock in their hundreds while the local unemployment rate skyrocketed. They were housed in the Orange Bowl Stadium, then transferred to the "tent city" under the knotted links of the interstate highway I-95 in Miami. The seventy-eight thousand who didn't have anyone willing to sponsor them were distributed among military bases, detention centers and prisons across the entire country. Pepe sees the matter from another perspective. He says that, within ten or twenty years, the Marielitos will forge a true American dream, becoming the future businessmen and professionals who will ennoble the Cuban-American community like the earlier émigré groups. But she has yet to see that dream materialize.

She abandons these digressions and begins a new cycle of phone calls, trying the only two neighbors' numbers she has in hopes of talking with her loved ones in Cuba. She can't reach the first and tries the second. When no one answers, she presses down with a finger the switch on which she should replace the receiver.

"I love you, Daddy," she whispers, the transmitter still against her chin.

She doesn't remember ever having spoken these words to her father. From now on, she'll say them more often, and he'll have to accept them instead of simply narrating the string of trifles that fill his boring days in Cuba. She doesn't know why she never realized, during her years as an arrogant and maladjusted teenager, how much Ángel did for the family, no matter what wagging tongues said. She was embarrassed by his drunkenness, yes — but it was he, for example, who gave her the reading bug through his old and modest *Reader's Digest* collection. With those articles and jokes, Emilia fought against boredom, imagined the world, and dreamed. And she owes him many other things that made her the woman she is today. Family has always been the most important thing for him. Emilia knows it. When her mother was seized by the terrible cancer that eventually claimed her, he couldn't have been a better husband. Nor a better father to her and her brother. He decided to stay in Cuba with them rather than take off with Mireya and Sofia, who had certainly become his new family.

Emilia goes down to the living room and pours herself another glass of wine, which she savors in front of the staircase as she listens to her husband and Abel's murmuring voices in the kitchen. Back in the study, she drinks to the health of the only great man in her life, sets the glass on the desk, and sits down. On Father's Day in Cuba, she used to give him a card along with a bottle of rum, the best she could afford. She didn't like it when he drank, but since she knew he would just get smashed anyway, the most she could do was guarantee that whatever he put into his body was something high quality rather than the rotgut improvised in Havana's tenements — not to mention the methylated spirits that had killed off so many. Her little bottle would still contribute to the same lethal end as the truly toxic stuff, but her father would enjoy a far more pleasant experience this way, from an aesthetic and sensory point of view. She promises to do whatever she can to get ahead — for herself, for him and for Eduardito.

"And of course I haven't forgotten you, dear Mama," she whispers to a framed picture on the desk. "If I had an address where I could send you a letter or a postcard and all my love, I'd do it right now. I wish you were here with me."

A few tears have slipped from her eyes. Blinking to clear her vision, she notices that a sparrow has appeared in the window. She wipes away her tears with the back of her hand and fervently wishes for a sign from her mother's elusive image after an absence of twenty years. The sparrow hops a couple of times on the windowsill and then takes flight.

Emilia rises to her feet and takes a few steps across the room. She has to raise her spirits. She had suggested to Pepe that they go and see a movie or a play yesterday, but — surprise, surprise — her husband claimed he was tired and had to prepare one of his talks. She wouldn't mind going to the theater in Coral Gables to feel the actors' presence on stage and listen to their clear diction from just a few short feet away. Or she could go to the movies and follow the characters to work, join them at the table, slip into their lives — into their beds, even, protected by the darkness of the projection room. But she needs real contact with real people. She's had enough of her co-workers' absent gazes and affected stiffness eight hours a day. She wouldn't say that her students at the institute where she teaches Spanish on two weeknights and Saturdays are exactly a sea of happiness, but at least they don't bore her. For the time being, she puts on a tape of old Cuban songs, the one she bought on 8th Street, and goes back downstairs for more wine.

As she heads upstairs again, she thinks she hears Abel saying goodbye. Seated at the desk once more and determined not to leave her refuge for a good while, she tries to write again, but the trumpets of the Conjunto Casino playing *"Llanto de luna"* make her emotional. She drains her glass and the music transports her to the workers' social clubs of the Marianao beaches, where the jukeboxes would churn out such songs over and over as she toasted herself in the sun.

> How to erase this long sorrow left by your farewell?
> How to forget you if inside, deep inside, you're still there?
> How to live this way, in this solitude so full of longing for you?

Music for drunk old men, people said back then. Now, glass in hand, a faint smile flits across her face.

*****

Stretched out on the sofa, Pepe rolls his second spliff. He lights it, tosses the lighter onto the coffee table, and settles into a corner. He starts thinking about how the American standard of living allows them to enjoy a quiet and safe home, but only on the surface: every possible form of security that their beautiful two-story, three-bedroom house in Little Havana affords them, every possible precaution they take inside and outside, are not enough to prevent the inexplicable and bizarre accidents that mark daily life — that merry-go-round with a missing screw where he watches himself turn circles. Will they be able to pay the rent? What horrific turn of events might await them around the corner? A crocodile could emerge from the sewers at any moment — not long ago, one of these creatures devoured a golfer in Palm Beach. A few days ago, meanwhile, several hospital patients died because the machines that maintained their vital signs were mistakenly disconnected by a custodian, and a motorcyclist was decapitated by a metal sheet that fell from a moving truck in one of those freak accidents. Not to mention the nutjobs who pick their victims at random. Besides, there's no time in this crazy life to even cook your food, let alone grow it — which is why, when you put anything into your mouth, you're exposed to anonymous farmers and workers and no one can ensure that there's not some weirdo among them who's capable of...

"Honey, put the pizzas in the oven when you go to the kitchen, please. I think I'm going to eat mine up here — I have a million things to do," Emilia says from the top of the stairs.

Pepe goes into the kitchen, lights the gas oven, and turns the knob that controls the flame to the midway point. He takes two prepackaged pizzas out of the refrigerator, tears open the plastic, and places them on sheets of aluminum foil before taking a long drag on the stub he's been holding between his lips all the while.

"Yes?" he hears Emilia respond upstairs. "Oh. How did I know it was you? How are things? ... Watch the pizzas; it's for me ... Sorry. I was talking to Pepe ... Yes ... Uh-huh ... You can't be serious ..."

Pepe grabs a jar from the spice rack, sprinkles the pizzas with oregano, and slides them into the oven. Bending down to peer through the see-through door as he adjusts the flame, he is suddenly terrified by the thought that the oven could explode mere inches from his face. It would make his eardrums leap; his cheeks would shatter. BAM! CRASH! BOOM! The explosion would shoot out metal splinters that would embed themselves in his ears and eat his brain. Don't be ridiculous, he scolds himself as he hears Emilia speaking on the phone.

"Uh-huh ... So there isn't ... So he doesn't ... So ... I see ..."

At this rate, it'll be another hour before she's off the phone, he estimates, convinced that the caller is the forty-something "workaholic" acquaintance who summarizes and types up medical records for a United Healthcare provider, as Emilia herself has begun to do in her free time. The woman talks nonstop and doesn't let anyone else get a word in edgewise. She's been coming to visit them almost every week since her husband was kicked to death by some mare he'd tried to have his way with, according to the gossip in Hialeah.

Pepe lowers the heat, picks up his joint from the countertop, and goes out to the patio, where he rediscovers his half-full glass of wine and downs it before bringing the no-longer-lit stub to his mouth. Weed is undoubtedly the drug that best agrees with him. He's flirted with others, even heroin, which helped him detach from everything for a while and concentrate on his ideas with a pleasant sense of warmth, but it's not really for him. When he had a more active political life and was hanging out in a group, he used to enjoy taking pills so he could sustain longer and wittier conversations. They gave him energy and good vibes. But that was then. Now they make him erratic. Now it's cocaine that induces the effect that most closely resembles what he misses about pills. He also fucks better and drives better and feels more elegant. The only downside is that it makes him sweat and clench his jaw — so much so that he's worried about damaging his teeth. You don't want to mess with your teeth if you don't have health insurance.

He thinks about all this as he returns to the kitchen to watch the oven. Facing the little door again, he recalls the story of the nanny who put two restless twins to sleep with gas. It's probably an urban legend, along with everything else, but he never ceases to be amazed by how crazy people can be. All he has to do is think of Marcelino, who calmly spent entire months outside La Alborada store in Havana, trying to sell his little aluminum cups to passers-by, only to end up here in Yankeeland burying a knife in a Nicaraguan's chest and slitting the guy's throat.

Compared with all those wackos, he considers himself pretty easygoing. The only "problem" he's had in his adoptive country was when he was fined for "driving a motor vehicle in a state of inebriation". Even though the car was parked in front of his house! He tried to explain to the officer that he'd had an argument with his wife, as happens in even the most harmonious of partnerships. He'd entered the vehicle sober and started drinking once inside — but he had absolutely no intention of driving. He'd only started the engine for the air conditioning and radio.

"These fucking rednecks are the squarest people around," he mutters. "Some neighborhood busybody must have called the police."

"Are those pizzas ready yet?" Emilia asks, appearing beside him and nearly startling him into sobriety.

*****

Back in her studio, pen in hand, Emilia sets out to review the draft of the article she's written this morning:

... Very few members of the Carter administration experienced the Camarioca crisis firsthand. Perhaps this explains why they didn't pay attention to Castro's repeated warnings; even at that point, he had already considered reopening the borders. In various reports, the CIA itself mentioned the possibility that large-scale migration might transpire. At first the government welcomed refugees, then rejected them, then released them onto the streets of Miami, then detained them. They dismissed the prospect of negotiating with Cuba altogether; a few days later, they suggested doing so on one condition: the naïve demand that Castro put an end to the exodus. The fact is that, by the time both parties took their place at the negotiating table, the "freedom flotilla" had already brought more than 125 000 Cubans to American territory. Statistics say that another 375 000 signed up to leave, but were ultimately unable to, so there is still a residue that could hardly be described as negligible. And it is precisely this residue that will allow Castro to reassert control over relations with the United States through the emigration valve, the demographic time bomb that we have already seen him use as a political weapon on previous occasions ...

She makes a few changes, brings the draft to the bedroom, switches on the lamp, and picks up the anthology of American short stories from the bedside table so she can rest her papers against it. She knows that Pepe will come to bed as soon as she's asleep and wake her up, without so much as a caress. Or maybe with that simian grip he applies with his toes, which she assumes should be taken as a playful pinch. She never knows whether her husband is tired or whether he simply wants her to disappear from his life. The saddest part is that he treats almost everyone with this same apathy as he becomes more and more of a hermit. If he didn't read the newspaper and still hold on to certain political concerns, he wouldn't be much different from Rip Van Winkle. What will he find when he wakes up? How much will his surroundings have changed? Will he be able to understand anything about this country that explodes anew with each passing second? The only thing missing will be the foot-long beard. And, to make matters worse, Emilia sometimes suspects that her husband has been bitten by the professional jealousy bug because of the small steps she's started to take with her opinion pieces in *El Cubanito*. Just what she needs!

*****

Meanwhile, perched on the edge of the sofa, bent over the coffee table, Pepe brings the end of a rolled-up bill to one of his nostrils. He knows this little shot is the only thing he needs to end the night on a high note: fucking his wife. He had to beg Abel to sell it to him. The ritual now performed, he picks up a copy of *El Nuevo Herald* and stretches out on the sofa, waiting for the effect to kick in.

His first sensation is a tickle in his right nostril. Then a drop of blood trickles out and falls onto the newspaper. He sniffs hard, jumps up from the couch, presses his nose between his thumb and index finger, and runs to the sink, breathing through his mouth. He faces the mirror, plugs the source of the problem with toilet paper, and tries to relax, certain that the bleeding will spontaneously stop within a couple of minutes. He's used to it, he tells himself, his head thrown back as he swallows what descends to his throat.

All Roads Lead to the Seawall

Four years after he was released on bail, Ángel was summoned for trial in the province's fourth judicial chamber. Then half a year passed before the verdict was issued. Despite the fact that he was declared innocent, he was told three months later to appear before the municipal court. The file wasn't there and they told him to await a new summons. He has now been waiting for almost another year, and he's even gone in person several times. They never deal with his concern.

Meanwhile, he continues to turn up punctually for his job at the workshop, as well as performing his guard duties and carrying out voluntary work as necessary — both for his own good and for Eduardito's. But he still fears that a sullen genie with flaming eyes will someday arise from this supposedly shelved affair and ruin everything. Should the gavel strike again, he might end up back in the clink. Nothing would surprise him after the story he's heard about a guy from Santiago who dreamed that he'd left Cuba on a boat with his family, told his friends about the dream in Parque Céspedes, and was arrested by State Security within a week for attempting an illegal departure from the country.

Tick-tock, tick-tock, tick-tock. Radio Reloj. Beeep. Six-fourteen. D'd'dee, d'd'dee. According to the radio news reader, during the decade now approaching its end, Halley's Comet has returned, one second has been added to the calendar year, smallpox has been eradicated, Spain has legalized divorce, the first artificial heart transplant has been performed, and the Human Genome Project has kicked off. The world is taking firm steps toward a new millennium. In Ángel's life, however, nothing seems to have changed. And the paralysis that leaves so much space for memories affects him more some days than others. Now, for example, as he waits for the milk to boil and the coffee to percolate, although he should return to the funeral wake for one of his co-workers, he opens the cupboard and takes out the bundle of letters Emilia has been sending him for years. He starts to read the most recent one, addressed to Eduardo and dated April 16, 1989, Miami Beach.

> ... I heard you've been very stubborn lately about this idea of leaving. Papi is worried even if he doesn't say so or show it. And he has more than enough reason to be worried. No matter how much I think about all this, I always reach the same conclusion: you need to be patient to stop yourself from doing anything crazy. But don't get discouraged. I've spoken with two different friends who can invite you to a third country ... Here Cubans live under a kind of permanent spell, enchanted by a Latin

American capital that was a swamp with no history before their arrival. They brag about being the only minority that earns as much money as the gringos, the most populous, the most politically powerful, blah, blah, blah. No one wants to hear about violence, corruption, racism, poverty, ignorance, or political intolerance ...

Ángel returns the letter to its envelope and picks another, sent almost ten years before from Little Havana along with the very first photos. It's one of his favorites. He has opened it, read it, reread it and refolded it so many times that it has begun to tear.

... I don't have trouble sleeping anymore. The chaotic thoughts that used to hit me in the early morning have completely disappeared. Sometimes what bothers me is waking up here when in my dreams I've been with all of you ... I always make an effort to forget the past and cling to the present, the new and eternal beginning: I try hard to make the street corners my own, and the same with the trees, the faces in the stores ...

Mafuco, the little dog Ángel rescued from the trash a couple of weeks ago, has slipped out of its cardboard box and run toward him, wagging its tail, and stepping on his shoes and pant cuffs. Ángel stands up to flee inactivity and his own thoughts, but he returns and sits down again after turning off the burner and pouring himself a cup of coffee. The heat feels extreme for May. He puts the pages of the letter back into their correct order, folds them, and carefully returns them to their envelope, along with the photos. He finds his cigarettes in a shirt pocket and lights one. Then he relaxes in the chair, watching the spirals of smoke as they fill the room.

Emilia's words have made him reflect on his life — pitiful, not only because it's no longer fueled by youth but also because it's stranded in desolation. He is nourished by memories alone while he blindly struggles to survive. Now, to make matters worse, the same letters that have provided a soothing, secret escape over the past nine years have begun to unsettle him, especially the most recent one. At first, Emilia would call almost every weekend and seemed happy with her good fortune: she had found work, she had access to all the books she'd always longed to read in Cuba, Pepe gave free rein to his political convictions without fear of ending up in jail, and, in general, they were doing very well. For some time now, though, her calls have become less frequent, and Ángel senses a certain dispiritedness in her letters.

And then there's Eduardo. The family circumspection that envelops everything related to Emilia means that Ángel often hides the truth from his son. Every letter, photo or phone call from the United States is radioactive material that could have a devastating effect if it reached the young man. As a father, Ángel believes that it's his responsibility to put up barriers if they help avoid catastrophe. A necessary evil. Unfortunately, any and all evidence from up north could be incinerated, injected into rock, frozen in polar icecaps, buried at the bottom of the sea or sent into orbit, and the boy's internal powder keg would still seem to be on the verge of explosion. The island paralyzes, torments, and Eduardo appears tired of waiting for a solution that would come from the leadership. Ángel understands his son perfectly, but he's afraid of losing him the way he has already lost Emilia.

The sunlight coming through the window grille illuminates part of the floor and the radio announces the time with the precision of an atomic clock. Beeep. Six twenty-five. D'd'dee, d'd'dee. Ángel gets to his feet and scans the lower part of the cramped unit he inhabits with his son, rent-free, in a foul-smelling tenement building: the little ovenless two-burner cooker, the refrigerator, the TV set, three dead cockroaches in a corner, the ordinary table, two chairs fallen into disuse — one stacked onto the other — and several piles of books atop the termite-eaten cupboard. The faint rustling of woodworms as they gnaw at the loft's floor and roof give him the impression that the place is on fire. It was only two years ago that he had painted the walls stunted by the wooden loft area, and grime has already consumed the white. The voices of the rebellious son and the exiled daughter coexist with the vestiges of a past that will never return. They constitute Ángel's only handle on life, and demand that he make a move, that he do something for the family.

"Papi, have you made coffee?" Eduardo asks from upstairs.

"Yeah, and there's boiled milk if you want," Ángel replies as he climbs the stairs. "What are you doing up at this hour?"

"Nothing, I'm just not sleepy. I have to be up early today anyway."

"Isn't your exam today?"

"Wednesday."

"Okay, so listen to me for a second. I have to go back to the wake. When you come back from school, if you can, buy some bread and eggs, and see if anything's come in at the fish store. I hope to be back before evening, but just in case."

As soon as the door is pulled shut, Eduardo gets to his feet and stretches. He leisurely makes his way down the wooden stairs, drops into a chair, stretches his legs, and lifts his gaze from the cockroaches to the cup of milk and coffee pot, avoiding the long fluorescent light that crackles insistently on the ceiling.

*****

The sun returns to heat everything up again, despite the fickle forms, clad in black and gray, threatening to conceal the sky.

"Stop messing around. Here come some of his family."

The guffaws incited by one of Migue's jokes are immediately stifled in coffee and smoke by a group of attendees at the wake in the funeral home. Alonso bites his cigarette and tries to make himself comfortable on a stool, his back to the café counter. During the memorial service, his thick gold chain gleaming on his white, hairy chest, he'll talk about the deceased's attitude toward life, his family, and his co-workers. For now, standing next to Ángel, he speaks in a measured voice about how old Papa was in top form, that he'd gotten himself an incredible mulatta chick, and that anyone can be unlucky enough to have the old ticker pack up.

*****

After reading aloud the objectives of her talk, the Linguistics professor begins to explain the relationship between form and content. Then she proceeds to the form of content and to that of form itself. Vladimir, miraculously present in the Zapata and G building at 7:30 in the morning, leers at the professor's buttocks — which wobble as she sketches the core of the conceptual structure on the blackboard — and gestures to Eduardo to take a look. The latter agrees, ogles too, and starts leafing through the novel Rafa has lent him. When hunger starts to overtake his enjoyment of the main character's glass-shattering capability, the bell rings, announcing a five-minute break.

Leaving the classroom, Eduardo sees the sweet little first-year mulatta by the stairs, leaning against the wall and smoking. Since it's a short break, he decides not to go to the cafeteria; instead, he'll go back inside, bum a cigarette, and come back out to ask for a light.

*****

The mourners gradually disperse around the Colón cemetery, filtering between marble tombs and headstones.

"He didn't seem like a bad person. Was he really a loan shark?" asks Marisa, the new girl in the workshop offices.

"That's what they say. Why lie to you? I even borrowed money from him on the odd occasion, in times of need. You know what it's like."

Ángel's words are interrupted by a tut from the young woman.

"What a shame I didn't know that sooner. I often find it hard to make it to the end of the month. That old Papa, may he rest in peace, would've gotten me out of a few tight spots."

Ángel doesn't know what to say. He starts contemplating how the blocks of narrow walkways combine to form larger squares which, in turn, are repeated in more or less the same pattern to create four vast areas, divided by the two avenues that cross at right angles at the chapel. Admiring its masterful design, he estimates the cemetery must easily occupy a fifth of a square mile.

Pancho and René join them in front of the chapel.

"There might be more people in this skyward-facing neighborhood than in all of Havana," Ángel says.

"The only place in Cuba where private property is respected. See how the family and society mausoleums are still there," Pancho adds.

The small group sets out along the avenue leading to the north gate, a section with elaborate combinations of granite, Carrara marble, glass and bronze. Beside a monument about seventy feet high, Marisa pitches to the group the last item of imported underwear she has to sell. Ángel listens to her soft, clear voice while he studies the shape of her breasts beneath her white blouse with an embroidered neckline. No one got paid today. If old Papa hadn't moved to this neck of the woods, maybe he could have loaned Ángel fifty pesos until he managed to collect his wages…

"Oh, Pablito's waving at me. Looks like he has room in his car. So no one's going to take the underwear?"

Ángel feels like an idiot simultaneously shrugging his shoulders and lifting his cigarette-holding hand to say goodbye to the girl, who runs toward a Plymouth 57 facing the arches of the enormous stone portico at the main entrance.

*****

The second half of the Linguistics lecture developed with half the class asleep and the other on the verge of passing out. It was followed by the Latin class, which often tended to become a lively intellectual debate, and today was marked by such translation gems as El Toro's "nutritive mother", Ana's "harvest of the day", and Juan Carlos's "birds of Caesar" that "died from lack of health". Eduardo wonders if he'll survive Scientific Communism, the course some wag has rechristened "Science Fiction". Still seated on a bench in the corridor, he watches his classmates enter the lecture hall. When he hears the professor announce they'll be continuing with the tenth topic, "communist education and multilateral personality development", he decides, in Marx's honor, to first fulfill his most basic need, which is to get something solid into his stomach. How? By taking advantage of the unsupervised dining hall in the building for students from the inner provinces at the junction of F and Third.

*****

Migue brings a cigarette to his lips, picks up a match and strikes it, but decides to speak before lighting up.

"Do you remember Castillo?"

"The face is familiar."

"I worked as a m-m-miller for a few m-m-months in Lombillo's workshop and I remember you."

"Ah, that's where I know you from!"

"You had an amazing girl right at your fingertips. Didn't you ask her out?" Migue asks this time.

"Well, you know, she's a high-maintenance chick and I'm stone-broke these days."

"Some other time, brother. Two bucks in your pocket and things change quick."

The same number of hours later, Migue will pour the last quarter-bottle of moonshine into three paper cups on one of the marble benches in La Piragua. Aware of the terrible day everyone has had, Castillo will work painstakingly to say that S-S-Saturday b-b-begins right then. As the sun sets, the shadow cast by the bottle will lengthen across the dusty white marble, and a catchy melody will reach them from the Hotel Nacional on the hill facing the sea:

Wood from a wrecked ship
Stone tumbling over itself
Aching heart roaming alone
From beaches and waves, that's me

*****

It's after six p.m. and Eduardo distributes dominoes across a bulletin board of the University Student Federation resting facedown on the players' knees. He is seated on a wooden box; the other three, on three lower bunks in a U-shape.

"Who's going first?" Héctor asks, giving Roberto a pointed look.

"You go ahead."

"Well, here's double tops," Héctor says.

Eduardo places his piece at a right angle to the starting double nine and watches Roberto put another one beside it.

At that moment, Raúl and El Flaco return with a bottle of rum, eager to replace the losers. Adrián doesn't think much about his next move and the game develops quickly on the 22nd floor as a fierce downpour hits outside.

As Raúl passes him the tin cup with rum in it, Eduardo wonders whether the stunning mulatta five floors down has finished studying. From what she told him during the break, she often comes to F and Third to study with her friends — and she's even slept there a couple of times when it's been too late for her to go home. It wasn't hard to convince her that going out is good for clearing the mind and helping information stick. She'll let him know once she's done, they've agreed, but she's far too attractive a mountain for Mohammed to assume that she'll come up to him. Mohammed will have to go down.

The snake of dominoes has grown so much that it now forms an "s" rather than a "j". Eduardo has two tiles left and it seems like luck is going his way.

"Here's an either-ender. Where do you want it, kiddo?" he asks Roberto, who doesn't rise to the provocation.

Without waiting for an answer, Eduardo kills Héctor's zillionth seven and sets the game to five. He stands up, not taking his eyes from the board. He silently counts the fives again and the only one that hasn't been played yet is the one clutched in his fist.

"I'm going out for a minute to do something no one else can do for me. Keep playing, I'll be right back."

He runs five floors down and the girl, who has finished studying and is now chatting with her friends, promises to go upstairs and get him shortly. Taking the stair steps two at a time, Eduardo returns to the floor where he has spent many evenings of his Classics degree fueled by rum and dominoes. Before heading back into the room, he decides to use the bathroom, where he hears his friends calling him: it's his turn to play and a girl is looking for him.

"I'm heading out. The rain's stopped," the girl says, intercepting him in the hall.

"Just hang on a mo and I'll be right back."

Puzzled and expectant, everyone stares at him, as, rather than taking his seat again, he hovers in the doorway.

"I'm afraid this is about it," he proclaims with false modesty before tossing his five-two onto the board.

"But this is a massacre!" El Flaco exclaims from an upper bunk, glancing at Roberto and Héctor's now revealed dominoes and seeing that the accumulated points, plus those from this round, will add up to more than a hundred.

"Too right it is," Adrián lets out as he stares incredulously at the tiles left to the losing pair.

"Holy shit!"

"He's totally fucked us over."

Adrián throws back his head and bursts out laughing with a thunderous slap on the board.

"And what do you think you're still doing with that pair of blanks? Did you see how they used them to make me pass? Now that's the last straw, man," Héctor reproaches his partner. "Didn't they teach you when you were a little kid that dominoes is a team game?"

"The last straw? Look who's talking: the guy who said he was 'lounging on the beach' before the game, and now it turns out that they had him passing twice with the blank. I don't know what language you're thinking in. Thinking? Huh-lo-oh!"

"Oh, don't give me that shit, man. Look at your tiles. You're left with that whole pile and you kill every seven I put on the table. The seven was my tactic and you fucked it up. You should have repeated it instead of killing it. No offense, but it takes an idiot to play like that."

"Idiot. Hahaha…" El Flaco laughs mockingly, choking on his rum.

"Says the amnesiac, that when…"

"Amnesiac. Hahahahaha," Adrián chimes in now, his guffaw ending in much coughing and juddering.

On another bunk, Raúl pounds the mattress and presses his face into the pillow. Fits of laughter seem to have infected everyone in the room, except for the losing pair. Eduardo makes use of the situation to slip through the door and grab the waist of the girl, who is waiting open-mouthed on the landing.

Two floors down, they can still hear the laughter.

*****

Ángel is halfway across the Avenida del Malecón. In an attempt to superimpose logical action on his body's fickle oscillations, he throws an interested glance at the monument to the American battleship whose mysterious explosion triggered the Spanish-Cuban-American War. He manages to discern the capitals on the two columns and then the architrave on which an imperial eagle had once rested.

Migue and the miller approach, but Ángel doesn't wait for them. With his paper cup half full of moonshine, he crosses the second half of the avenue until he reaches the esplanade by the seawall and strikes out toward the US Interests Section and the Parque Martí, the sea to his right.

He makes use of the walk to have a chat with himself. He's not a lucky guy. He seems to struggle more than anyone else to solve his own problems and doesn't have a cent to his name. Migue has always played the fool and, when he poured the last round from the second bottle, he made it clear he didn't have any money to spare. Castillo doesn't know him well enough to lend him any, despite having said that it was his turn t-t-today and theirs t-t-tomorrow. In any case, what for? Well, to eat tomorrow and to buy cigarettes, to treat Marisa to something, to have a bet and try to turn things around, he answers himself before he starts to curse old Papa, who always went round in circles before he'd loan him peanuts. That piece of shit who never actually resolved anything for anyone.

"Hey, wait for us!" he hears far behind him.

He tries to control the long strides that bring him toward the avenue, strains to look back without slowing down, and sees Migue and Castillo turn to sweet-talk two brown women crossing alongside them.

"Listen here, bonbons, you're gonna melt in the sun. Why don't you walk in the shade?" Migue murmurs smoothly.

"Are those capitalist pants, by any chance? Because they've got the masses real oppressed," Castillo adds.

After a brief pause, the miller brings his hands to his head and concludes, "I'd like to be one of those panties so I could be all tight and stuck in there. Even if I get farted to death!"

Uneasy, the women pretend they haven't heard him. They look at each other, give the men a sidelong glance, and walk off swinging their hips provocatively.

*****

Eduardo and the girl leave the Parque Martí behind, and advance toward the US Interests Section and the Hotel Nacional. To their left, the pom-pom clouds and fine reddish bands in the sky melt into the tranquil sea and invite them to sit on the seawall.

Eduardo shares the opinion that all efforts to teach students to acquire knowledge on their own are inadequate. At the same time, his gaze tries to take in the girl's violet blouse, green-checkered cotton skirt and black canvas shoes, gracefully crossed over the wide cement dike, miraculously dry after the downpour. Although her brown eyes emphasize why students remain unmotivated, her bold stare provokes in Eduardo an uncontrollable tingling sensation.

"What's clear is that everything's bad, very bad, as bad as it can get, in the worst way possible," he says, theatrically shaking his head, in an allusion to one of the books she needs to study for her exam.

The girl smiles without dropping her gaze or pulling back so much as a fraction of an inch. The sea breeze returns to sweep her long coppery hair across her cheeks, tinted a suggestive mamey-fruit color, which in turn accentuates the mystery in her eyes. Eduardo catches her womanly fragrance in counterpoint with the one left behind by the rain.

"Bad, very bad, as bad as it can get, in the worst way possible," Eduardo repeats, this time in the tone of voice that mothers use with their babies.

A few seconds ago, he didn't dare to steal a kiss even though it seemed to be the perfect moment. Now he leans forward and touches her full lips with his own, and she responds. He can feel himself levitate for an instant before surrendering to a free fall of intoxicating caresses. The afternoon wanes.

*****

Ángel keeps fighting against the uncontrollable swinging of his legs until the paper cup makes a dull noise in his right hand and the moonshine wets his chest. An egg is frying in the palm of his hand. Sparks leap between his head and the rough concrete of the intruding wall, which has taken on a life of its own and comes crashing down on him.

He manages to stand up and notes the orange reflection the sun has left over the horizon. He reckons it's too late to go to Felo's and bum some food. Besides, he did that yesterday. His brother can go to hell, too! With his forearms leaning against the concrete, he watches the waves buffet some sticks about on the rocks. The swaying dizzies him. How to vomit over the edge of a yard-thick wall?

And where has Eduardo come from this time? God bless him!

The Key

The American cars from the '50s sputter along San Lázaro street, where posters commemorating historic events or urging people to die or make other sacrifices related to the revolutionary process confront the crowds at the bus stops. Turning right into Aramburu, Eduardo enters an area of collective deterioration marked by features very familiar to him: a bricked-up arch here, a sealed-off window there, potholes in the street, and metal work with rusty arabesques dividing emaciated balconies.

He's reached his destination after an exhausting walk in the sun, but the silence and tranquility unsettle rather than soothe him. He feels watched. He hesitates a moment, then overcomes his timidity and enters the dark, high-ceilinged mansion now transformed into tenements.

The building, divided into countless rooms, has been abandoned to its own resistance. At the end of the wide central hall, several shirtless men shuffle around silently, carrying water buckets. On the right, a mass of electrical cables, covered in a crust of dirt, receives him and guides him up a broad marble staircase, which he climbs, supporting himself against the iron banister missing its handrail.

Upstairs smells of boiled clothes and Madonna lilies, and Eduardo can hear a bolero. He recognizes Orlando Contreras's voice from one of those old records his father still keeps. There's always someone who dares to blast the music of singers loathed by the authorities, he muses. But then he shrugs off these ideas, knowing all too well that inexplicable situations constantly arise on the island — like his own presence in this building.

It's not hard to find the door that had been described to him: the second on the right, painted blue. As soon as his fingers make contact with the small, sturdy knocker set against the peeling paint, one of the door leaves swings open.

"Come in, come in," his lovely mulatta hurries to whisper. She kisses him on the mouth after closing and bolting the door. "Coffee?"

"Sure."

"You didn't see an old Chinese woman downstairs, did you?"

"No. Why?"

"No reason. It's just that the people here spend their whole lives nosing into everyone else's business, gossiping about who comes in, who goes out, and what you're doing every second of the day."

Who comes in and who goes out. And what does that have to do with him? Eduardo lights a cigarette, although he hasn't seen an ashtray around. The girl hands him the coffee in a short glass and gestures for him to flick the ash into it. Eduardo sits down on one of the two chairs beside the table. From where he is seated, he can see a set of pine shelves full of piled-up cardboard boxes and shoes spilling out of them, part of the staircase leading to a wooden loft area, and a mirror that has lost half its silvering but which nonetheless seems to widen the ten-by-twelve-foot room.

The coffee is unsweetened, but Eduardo drinks it anyway and returns to his cigarette as he watches her move toward the kerosene burner on the tiny countertop. Her honey-colored hair stands out against her loose white shirt, which appears to be the only thing covering her body.

"Where should I empty this?" asks Eduardo, putting out the cigarette in the cup.

"Here," she responds in a warm voice, pointing to a yellow plastic bucket under the sink.

"Can I use your bathroom?"

"It's outside and it's shared," she warns. "You have to go downstairs and all the way to the back. Number one or number two? If it's number one and you can't hold it, use this bucket."

The most-desired mulatta at school teasingly motions beneath the sink again, which has neither a siphon nor a waste pipe.

"It's just to wash my hands. I don't like the smell these cigarettes leave on my fingers."

"Come, wash them here."

Eduardo stands and takes a couple of steps toward her, ash-flecked cup in hand, while his gaze takes in her tawny hair and the womanly shape beneath her garment. The girl, who seems perfectly comfortable with the silence and his insistent stare, turns and takes Eduardo by the waist. He suddenly finds himself without the glass and caressing her hips, torso and firm breasts under the cotton.

The shirt sweeps over her hair. Eduardo's kisses and nibbles move from her mouth to her cheeks, her perfumed neck, her cinnamon breasts and their hard, bud-like nipples. His hands fill with the roundness of her smooth, cool buttocks, and with a moist, tangled jungle. He kneels, but she takes him by the hand and leads him to the table before climbing onto it, pulling him gently by the shoulders toward her and leaning back. Chaotically, Eduardo kisses her inner thighs, yanks off his pullover and a shoe, and shakes one leg out of his pants. She sits up, runs her fingers through his hair while kissing him softly, and lets him drop into one of the black iron chairs upholstered in red vinyl. She then climbs onto the chair and places her feet alongside his thighs. Holding onto the back of the chair, she begins to ride him at a wild, passionate pace, which grows frenetic in no time at all. So frenetic that Eduardo thinks he's starting to lose his sight.

"Shh," she hisses through her slightly rounded lips, close to Eduardo's.

The two of them remain motionless in a chilling silence. A key has entered the lock but it fails to open the door. Their heavy breathing and pounding hearts make it difficult to hear clearly. Eduardo is startled to feel an internal shuddering, followed by a spasm, and helplessly surrenders to his orgasm. The girl dismounts and approaches the door on tiptoe. He watches her long hair draped over her brown shoulders. A fine hollow runs down the center of her back to a waist tapering just enough to set off the most sensual hips. A thread of semen stretches downward between her sculpted thighs.

*****

Before reaching the landing, Eduardo glances covertly in several directions but doesn't see any old Chinese women. Nor does he notice anything strange downstairs. As soon as he's out on the sidewalk, his instinct for self preservation tells him that he should quicken his step and not look back.

A few blocks down San Lázaro, he makes sure he's not being followed. Just in case, he turns right into Soledad, left into Ánimas, right and left again, and ends up on Belascoaín, where he's suddenly dazzled by the light of an afternoon that strikes him as perfect for walking and giving himself over to oblivion. He could easily vanish into one of the movie theaters in the area, he thinks, as he proceeds toward Zanja, but the Favorito and Cuatro Caminos are the only ones left. A couple of years back, he could have gone to the Palace, Wilson, Edén, Oriente, Astor, Miami or Belascoaín. Instead, he should cross and go down San Rafael, where he'll have the Duplex and the Rex. Or *would* have had. What's the deal with these movie theaters closing their doors, one after another, falling into a decay that will inevitably end in collapse? Of the hundred-plus cinemas he used to see in the listings, only around twenty remain.

He certainly isn't lacking in eagerness to go for a six-peso mug of beer on the corner, but he continues for another long stretch until he reaches Galiano, where he feels the sea's presence on his left. Sunlight floods the intersection, which is thronged with women coming and going — shopping, he supposes, although he can't imagine who might want the crude, mostly useless items on display in the store windows. He grew up hearing store names like the Ten Cent on Galiano street, El Encanto, Flogar, La Moda, La Época, Fin de Siglo, J. Vallés and El Bazar Inglés. When he was little, his father would take him to many of these stores to buy stamps, a baseball glove, a shirt or a pair of shoes. But now he has no idea how many are still open. For Eduardo, Havana is a cemetery for more than cinemas — stores, theaters and factories are buried here, too. The capital and the island itself are a cemetery for hopes.

The important thing now is to get lost in the sea of people circulating along the San Rafael boulevard in all directions, he tells himself, zigzagging swiftly among Cubans of all races and tourists in hats and caps. He crosses the Parque Central, where a dozen men argue about baseball around a marble bench in the shade, and heads down Obispo. He leaves a couple of bookstores behind, as well as a modernist façade, a pharmacy, and a bar or two. Then he skirts the Plaza de Armas on the left, across the wooden paving, hops over to Segundo Cabo Palace to savor the cool of the colonnade, and proceeds toward Avenida del Puerto through a narrow, shady street.

Standing on the sidewalks and asphalt, the patrons of a bar lift their jars and make the most of the breeze wafting in from the bay. As soon as Eduardo sets foot on the sidewalk, he's approached from the right by the figure of a man with his hands behind him. Eduardo tries to pull away, but immediately receives a sharp blow to the groin and finds himself face-to-face with his Asian-featured attacker. His gesture as he tries to protect himself from the bloodied knife earns him another stab near the right lung. He's shocked by the intensity of the pain. Then the steel blade sears his left cheek. The drinkers distance themselves as best they can from the assailant, a shadow vanishing toward the port.

Eduardo hasn't had time to struggle and defend himself. He shudders and takes a few clumsy steps, supporting himself against the wall and leaving blood stains as he goes. The horrified atmosphere in the bar makes him wonder fleetingly whether his wounds could be fatal. Will he end up buried in this dirty city, just when he has so much left to do?, he asks himself as he falls to the ground. He feels no pain but rather a sudden sense of wellbeing, a feeling of lightness and calm. His internal cavities lend further resonance to the sound of his back hitting the pavement and his eyes show curious onlookers an expression of astonishment in an empty gaze.

Terrified screams rise up among the observers who have crowded around the prostrate body in the road.

"My God!"

"What a stab, right in the stomach!"

"Stop a car, goddammit, or he'll bleed to death right here!"

Someone has stopped a Lada 1600 with state plates by planting themselves in front of it on Avenida del Puerto. Several men carry Eduardo's motionless body. As blood bubbles up on the right side of his ribcage, he is struck by a series of images and thoughts, all melting together in a sweet light. Either time is slowing down or his mental processes are speeding up. Then his senses go dull and he simply floats in a vast grayish corridor.

In the closest surgical hospital, Hilda's pale figure lovingly assures him that he's dead even though the medical staff insist on resuscitating him. He longs to stay in his mother's company, immersed in this extraordinary reality, but from within his peaceful abandon he suddenly hears, like a brutal metallic buzz, chunks of conversation: "pneumothorax", "hemorrhage", "drainage".

Ships in the Night

It's ten o'clock and he's hungry. Will he be able to sleep, or will his empty stomach keep him up? He's got Faulkner and Quiroga under the pillow. He grabs the latter. From the 1954 Crosley tabletop radio beside him and synched to the American station WGBS, he listens to the Alan Parsons Project. He finds his own recovery after only forty days miraculous, although he is still under total bed rest.

He was lucky to have been attended to as soon as he reached the hospital. They had examined him and sent him into surgery immediately, managing to halt the peritonitis caused by the stab wound in his colon. In the following days, relatives, friends, neighbors and fellow students started filing through the recovery room. And after two weeks under observation at the hospital, with constant IV and frequent wound care, he was officially discharged to continue the healing process at home.

But he's tired of visitors. He thinks he flatters them by just lending an ear; that must be why they stay so long. No one would believe him, but what he most wants at the moment is to go back to university. And he will soon, if his recovery carries on at this pace.

His eyes wander across the loft area. An Underwood typewriter case. The York air-conditioner that serves as a bedside table. A three-speed General Electric radio record player, console-style, apparently broken but with a fine wooden cabinet. On top of the record player, a plastic

Soviet fan that seems to be the only functioning object around, aside from the Crosley. It only works at one of its three speeds, with aluminum blades Ángel fashioned himself.

His father fixes this old junk little by little as best he can, hoping to earn a few extra pesos. He has also hung a string of garlic heads up here, instead of in the kitchen, so that no one gets any ideas. "You can't buy garlic anywhere in Havana," were his words when he appeared with them in hand. Right now he's downstairs, watching Fidel's speech on TV. From the single bed in the loft, Eduardo can hear his old man protesting and pictures him taking a swig of alcohol with every pause in his dissenting remarks. Sometimes he hears the sound made by the glass when Ángel sets it down on the oilcloth or granite. Eduardo feels that — except for these long weeks of convalescence — he has coexisted but never really shared much with his father. And this leaves him with a sour taste in his mouth. His apparent lack of filial affection makes him feel uncomfortable, especially now that Ángel has stopped working and become a devoted nurse.

Barry Manilow's voice emerges from the old Crosley, singing of a love that's comfortable at a distance and of two ships passing in the night. Eduardo lifts his gaze to the ceiling planks, which rest crosswise along wooden beams separated two hand spans and supported in turn by a thick beam embedded in the wall. All together, the frame reminds him of a boat with the keel facing up.

Beauties on Duty

Today the "duty officer" is supposed to be the Latin professor, but he called to say he won't be in because his daughter is sick. Eduardo has reported to the "Garrison".

He closes the main door of the building from the inside, and stretches out on a wooden bench by the entrance, enveloped in the empty early-morning silence that fills what is normally the school's busiest space during the day.

The mandatory student watch falls to him about every two months in strict rotation. He understands that it's yet another of the small actions that help make Cuba a safe, well-organized country, but it's also a stone in his shoe. One of many that mark his existence. How many hundreds of these guard duties has he been on so far? And how many more will he have to perform? Before he's finished asking himself this second question, a strange arousal takes over his body. It's the silence that throws up these mind tricks, he thinks, getting to his feet and heading toward the restrooms.

He decides to enter the women's room, where the pink of the tiles instantly transubstantiates into Miriam's breasts. He hasn't finished stroking them before he starts to bite Elena's thighs and then to caress the secretary's pretty little ass. Swept up in a whirlwind of pleasure, these beautiful faces redden, their lips part, and they demand Eduardo's kisses. He contorts sideways in front of the mirror, with the horizontal two-inch scar that stretches all the way to his nostril turned toward the half-open doors. The inscrutable Semiotics professor melts with every obscenity he whispers to her. The first-year Vietnamese girl shouts in ecstasy and unleashes an untamable force. Ana, Cristina, Esteban's girlfriend and the sophisticated Dean all receive his onslaughts, and this last one is generously attended to in the hollow of his palm.

Boca Ciega

Suddenly remembering the previous day's incident in downtown Havana, Ángel springs up from his seat in a sweat. He thinks for a moment about the party on the beach he's been invited to. Perhaps he could leave the city for a day or two to calm down and sketch out a plan to disappear completely.

He goes upstairs and cools himself off on the outside with a bucket of water and an aluminum cup.

Then, sitting back at the table with a copy of *Granma* dated Saturday, August 6, 1994, "36th Year of the Revolution", he cools off on the inside with the beer he's bought in a clandestine bar. It's not hard to find the special weekend listing for the two TV channels in the two-page newspaper: a broadcast of the event supporting the Revolution at La Punta called "Fidel for Life", the Commander-in-Chief's appearance on the program "Today", an account of the funeral services conducted in the Plaza de la Revolución and Guantánamo for the lieutenant murdered during the second hijacking of the boat *Baraguá*, a summary of Fidel's activities during his visit to Colombia, a broadcast of the memorial service at Mariel, and the Camaguey community's posthumous tribute to the ship lieutenant.

Beer in hand, he closes the paper. On the front page, Fidel emphasizes that the United States bears full responsibility for the mass migration that will inevitably be unleashed. Old actions and old words try to justify a situation that Ángel has already experienced in prior spin cycles. His thoughts flee to his family's recent history. He can't remember what he'd wanted for himself and for his children. He's gone adrift somewhere during the long search, but he refuses to accept his fate. The priority now is for the three of them to reunite and take care of each other, especially now that Emilia has divorced and probably isn't in the best of spirits. Maybe this new agitation along the coast means it's the right time to leave the island once and for all — before he starts to lose his nerve. The good thing is how bad it's all getting, he tells himself as he downs his beer and stands up.

Still absorbed in his plot, he pours Mafuco a bowl of water beside the staircase. If he has to start offloading ballast, he thinks he's found the puppy a home with the little boy and divorced mother who live at the back of the tenement. They seemed willing to take him the other day.

*****

Four couples move their bodies to the beat of taped music by the Orquesta Revé. As part of the dance, a mulatto's hip thrusts against the groin of a twenty-something woman with very white skin and short, bleached hair.

"I think the chubby one likes you."

Ángel, who has been scanning the room's damp-stained walls before resting his gaze on the flaking paint of the entry hall ceiling, takes a moment before responding to Migue's words.

"Did she say something to you?" he finally articulates with a tired delay.

"No, but it's not like she had to. Careful, here she comes."

As soon as she reaches the beat-up wicker sofa, the girl settles in next to Ángel with a "Shove over a bit that way".

She quickly continues, "I don't know what's gotten into that one," nodding toward the woman with bleached hair, who's just seized the mulatto's neck in her arms and, with her torso firmly affixed to his, smilingly lifts her feet from the ground.

"She's really got it, hasn't she, pal?" Migue remarks with malicious sarcasm as he offers his friend a cigarette.

Ángel lights it and watches as Migue's Miami-based cousin approaches, a woman of around thirty, slim, olive-skinned, her hair dyed black. She comes and sits on the armrest of the sofa, then leans forward toward the "chubby one" and shouts into her ear.

"I joked to Carmen that I'd slept with half the men here and she says she's gonna do all of them today."

"What's up with her?"

"Don't let her know I said anything but she's tripping on pills."

Migue's cousin turns to Ángel. No sooner has she asked him if he'd like to dance than she is forced to leave her tall zinc cup with him when a rangy, effeminate man takes her by both hands and leads her onto the dance floor.

Ángel places the cup on the floor between his feet and takes a swig of red wine from his own chipped, blue-enameled cup. He then seeks out the intense gaze of this Carmen, who's shot a couple of interested glances toward the sofa during the dance. The music stops and people remark that she's gone into one of the bedrooms with the mulatto.

As the gossip and complicit smiles spread through the house, Ángel watches Migue's cousin sit on the low wall between the porch and the garden, fidget with a pack of cigarettes, and settle one bare thigh across the other. She bears a startling resemblance to Mireya: the same long, well-toned legs, small breasts and mysteriously sensual lips. When he manages to catch her eye, Ángel is planning to raise his eyebrows and make a face expressing a kind of sympathy for her obligations to the whole affair: she's the one who rented the beach house and bought, in dollars, all the food and drink here. In this way, an unspoken understanding will take root between them. Too bad those thighs have now shifted into a less revealing pose. But it's not the end of the world, he consoles himself, taking a long swig of wine and returning the little enameled cup with wine sediment to its place on the floor.

The music starts up again: one of the popular Van Van songs. Various couples make a circle and start to dance, showing off simultaneous, copycat dance steps. The *rueda de casino* salsa movements are like another world to Ángel; he's never understood them. He has no trouble following the series of steps as long as the dancers stay in one place, but their deft spins as they move from one spot to the next make him dizzy just from watching. Someone shouts "lie" and the others reverse the last command as if rewinding a movie; then that someone says "double" and they all repeat the step. Ángel is amazed by how, within minutes, people who are probably strangers can understand each other perfectly through the art and grace of dance.

He feels a bit groggy from the mix of drinks, hunger and the complicated turns under the arches formed and broken, with dizzying speed, by the dancers' arms. He's jolted into alertness by their collective clap and forward stamp following the command to "kill the cockroach". Then he sees three teenage boys come through the front entrance with two girls in garish makeup. The quintet are encouraged to go to the kitchen and get themselves a drink just as Carmen emerges from the bedroom, her head held high and a cigarette in her mouth. Running her hands through her hair, she affectionately greets the newcomers and hooks one of the boys, a hefty blond, around the waist as the mulatto comes out of the bedroom with his afro hair disheveled.

"Look! He's cutting in line!" the chubby girl shrieks to direct the attention of two young men toward Carmen's return to the bedroom with the blond boy, the two now holding hands.

Ángel walks out to the entrance, where he sees Migue walking slowly, glass in hand, across the grass. The starry night with its cool breeze in the company of a friend to chat and enjoy a drink with strikes him as a whole lot more appealing than subjecting himself to heat, music at full blast and the excesses of mindless young people.

"Did you have any trouble finding this place?" Migue asks.

"Nope. The directions you gave me were fine."

"Well, man, I missed the stop and had to walk for miles. Almost all the way from Guanabo. But here we are. It's not every day you can enjoy a beach house, huh?"

"You're telling me. An hour ago I was roasting in Havana and now it feels nice and cool here. Wonderful."

"Speaking of Havana, have you heard how things are heating up? Yesterday, people took to the streets downtown."

"Shit, man! I haven't told you anything yet. Yesterday I happened to go past La Punta and it was all going on."

"Like what? What did you see?"

"What did I see? Well, first, a big group of kids and some older guys on bikes and on foot. They came out from all directions and hollered 'Freedom, freedom, down with Fidel!'. The cars passing on Avenida del Malecón honked in support." Ángel's cheeks start to flush. "And then some trucks showed up with some really burly guys who got out and immediately started beating the hell out of everyone. People didn't hold back: they shouted 'Sellouts!' and threw stones at them. I heard things got rough in Parque Maceo, too. The armored BTR dispersed the crowd with water cannons and there was an anti-aircraft gun aimed at the balconies. Imagine how the people living in those buildings must have felt, with soldiers on their street, aiming at their houses."

"And what did you do?"

"My friend, I can't say that I got into a fight with the police, but I did yell really loud with the others and shoved a dumpster in front of the Deauville Hotel to cut off the ones chasing the kids." Ángel catches his breath before carrying on. "Then I looked for a number 20 bus to wrap up a job I'd left half finished. But the crowd went all the way downtown and destroyed the display windows of who knows how many dollar shops."

"Must have been a big thing!" Migue exclaims. "My neighbor's son was arrested and taken to a police station in Jaimanitas because the ones in downtown Havana and Old Havana were full to bursting."

Around midday, when Ángel had to stop repairing a water pump in Vedado to go in search of a diestock, he noticed several dozen men arranging themselves into compact groups in the park on 25 and C. Strong men, like the ones he'd seen on the Malecón. They were wearing white pullovers with the red logo of the Blas Roca Calderío construction brigade. And they were carrying sticks and rods. He mentions the incident to Migue, who listens intently and adds:

"Things must be pretty ugly if not even *Granma* tries to cover them up."

Ángel knows this very well. He's been following the events in the press, in conversations on the street and in person. The most alarming episode occurred early in the morning on July 13, when around seventy people took an old tugboat out of the Havana port in order to leave the country. Chased, rammed and attacked with hoses by three ships, the tugboat sank less than ten miles from the coast. The death toll: thirty-seven, including ten children. On July 26, a day of official celebrations, another group hijacked the passenger boat *Baraguá* in Havana Bay. Two days later, there was a similar hijacking. This time it was *La Coubre*, which was conducting its normal journey with over eighty people aboard. Then they took the *Baraguá* a second time — the incident in which the officer died and the authorities captured the hijackers, who had run out of fuel. The government reinforced surveillance at the ferry dock of Muelle de Luz, changed the bus stops along Avenida del Puerto, and suspended all passenger transport in the bay.

Hundreds of Havana residents swarmed through the area at all hours and, yesterday, as Ángel has just told Migue, they attacked the storefronts.

"But I still haven't told you the worst part."

"You mean there's more?"

"Check this out," Ángel starts again. "This morning, I turned on the TV, and guess what I saw. Or, worse still, who I saw. Myself pushing the dumpster! I have a feeling that they're going to pulverize me if I go back to the neighborhood. I wish I could sleep here tonight, even if it's on the roof. Failing that, on a lifeguard chair or even the sand. Mosquitoes and all."

"I hear you, brother."

"What I want right now is to disappear. And I'm even more worried about Eduardito. That kid's going to hop on a raft with the worst of the worst, right when I least expect it. It's keeping me up at night. I swear I'd give anything to get him out of the country. Whatever it takes — because, if not, he's going to follow his own unreliable head."

"I totally understand. Now listen. Thinking seriously about all this, now that you've opened up to me, and that's why friends have to talk about things, there's a possibility I've been mulling over, but I don't have the money for it."

"And what's that possibility, if you can tell me?"

"It has to stay between us."

"Don't worry."

"Remember how we had a couple drinks with Castillo on the Malecón the day of old Papa's burial?"

"How could I forget?"

"I don't know if you knew that he lives in Santa Fe and has a little fishing boat."

"No, I didn't know."

"Well, when you took off on your own that day, he told me he wanted to sell the boat for five thousand dollars, payable directly to him or to his sister in Barcelona — she's applied for reunification and wants to bring him to Spain.

I'll get to the point: if you and your son pay thirty-five hundred between the two of you, I can guarantee the other fifteen, and the three of us can get out on that boat, which is in pretty good shape. Opportunity doesn't knock twice, brother. Eduardo's recovered from his operation by now, right?"

"Completely, thank God. But, Migue, where am I going to get that kind of money when I'm flat broke?"

"Forget the money for the time being and tell me what you think of the plan. No bullshit. Let's say that your daughter can solve the money problem. If she wants to get you two out of here, she'll move heaven and earth to come up with it. Then you guys can pay her back when you start working."

"The truth is, the way you describe it, it sounds perfect. But I don't know if Emilita can get that kind of cash. I'd also have to sit down with Eduardo and talk father to son, or man to man."

"Rest easy, buddy. You do what you have to do and we'll talk again this coming weekend. But just think — quite by chance, or the hand of God, or whatever you want to call it, my cousin happens to be here at this very moment. She's totally trustworthy and is going back to Miami soon. She could easily talk with Emilia face to face. The only thing we need is for your daughter to hand over the money to Castillo's sister and then we'll be crossing the pond. On a respectable boat and not a fucking little raft!"

"You must introduce me to your cousin later."

"No problem," Migue reassures his friend, leading him to the middle of the traffic-free road. "Over the next few days, I'll scrounge some gas and other things we'll need. Just the three of us — no one else, okay? Man, I wouldn't trust my own shadow with something like this, but you're my brother. Don't let me down. Deal?"

"Deal."

"Quietly, okay?"

"'And somewhat indirectly, because, to achieve certain objectives, they must be kept under cover; to proclaim them for what they are would raise such difficulties that the objectives could not be attained'," Ángel proudly finishes the Martí quote.

"Exactly."

They shake hands to seal the pact.

"Now we're on our way," Migue adds with a schoolteacher's tone, a glimmer of excitement in his eyes, and his face turned skyward. "The stars will guide us at night, but the first thing we have to do is find an easy-to-locate constellation, like Ursa Major. Can you find the shape of a plough or a dipper?"

"That one, right?"

"Exactly. Look carefully now while the sky's clear. If you draw an imaginary line between the two brightest stars in the dipper, and you lengthen it about five times over, you'll find the North Star. That's the one we need if we can't come up with a compass. Is your glass empty? Let's go inside."

Just as the two men enter the living room, an inner door opens and a scantily-clad Carmen parades out, wearing her shoes like flip-flops and with an unlit cigarette in her left hand. She's increasingly translucent to Ángel's eyes, her skin revealing the green veins in her arms and legs. The girl pauses briefly in front of two dark-skinned men who are standing in a corner talking. She exchanges a few sentences with them before proceeding toward the kitchen. On her way back, smiling, the cigarette now lit between her lips, she throws her arms around their waists and leads them to the bedroom, the bottle-green door slamming shut behind them.

With eyes soaked in drunkenness, Ángel reckons that the pale girl has gone to bed with four men in under an hour. Then he stops to think about how quickly he himself has acquiesced to Migue's proposal. He doubts there's anything tricky about it — his friend just wants to solve his own problems. And he's aware that he won't come up with a better partner than Migue for the journey on the whole island: besides knowing how to sail, he is discreet, intelligent, and follows an honor code hard to find these days.

"Who else? You? No, you already went. And so did you."

The effeminate man takes evident pleasure in organizing a line. In order to get back to Havana tonight, Ángel remembers, he'd have to leave while the buses were still running. But he's determined to stay in Boca Ciega, at least for tonight. If possible, the whole weekend. It's a shame he can't take Castillo's boat right from here.

"And you?"

Migue gets in line and, to avoid trouble, Ángel agrees to follow him if the fornication machine wishes it so. How is it that these fellows, all full of youth, can emerge exhausted from the bedroom, shake hands, smile, and shout "Oh yeah!", "Incredible!" and "Oof!" with such astonishing ease? In any case, eating where so many others have been nibbling at the food, so to speak, is the last thing he really feels like doing. But who knows if he's the one who, at fifty-four, has to come and shut them all up with an exemplary performance — and end up with a bed and a roof over his head as spoils of war? The Mambo King. Will he be up to the job at his age, with hunger churning in his body and his mind in a spin?

Minutes later, after watching Migue enter the bedroom, Ángel returns to the porch, tosses another cigarette butt into the street, and wonders if Emilita had gone to parties like this in her youth or at the beginning of her promising career as a teacher. She's a married woman now — and divorced, he corrects himself — but who knows? How committedly Hilda had tried to teach her daughter so many things! The fantasy that flowed through so many sacrifices!

The close friends they could have become! He tries to imagine how much his life might have changed if he'd gone through Mariel with Mireya, or through Camarioca in '65, when his sister-in-law came to fetch them. Hilda gave the answer she had decided was most convenient, because she knew she was on borrowed time with that wretched lung cancer and didn't want to be a burden to her sister. The doctors were confident about an antibody therapy that would go directly to the tumor but, when Ángel looked at the skeletal patient with her head shaved, crawling with tubes, it wasn't the same woman from several months before. Sedated but fully conscious, the poor woman didn't miss a single detail of her own decline. Until she no longer recognized her children and began shouting insults, tearing off her clothes, and pulling out her IV and oxygen supply. Perhaps it was better for everyone when her organs started to fail, one after another, all in the same day, and her body completely shut down after a final gasping breath.

"Pssst."

The music has stopped and all eyes spring to Ángel, who instinctively walks down the front steps toward the grass.

"Where are you going?" the chubby girl shouts.

"I'll be right back. I'm going to take a walk," he answers uneasily.

"Pssst."

Ángel decides to quicken his step and, as soon as he hears someone behind him doing the same, breaks into a run.

Secrets

Ángel breaks the tip of a Reloba cigar with his thumbnail and finishes blunting it with his teeth. He observes it for a moment, brings it to his mouth, bites it and draws from it at a right angle to the flame of a match. It doesn't fully catch, so he blows gently and turns the cylinder until the ember glows evenly across the circular end. As well as the Reloba and family-sized box of matches, he's brought a large aluminum cup of coffee for the guard duty as a member of the Committee for the Defense of the Revolution. His son is content with a book and the portable Meridian radio.

"Just getting started with this other job in the museum and I've already been saddled with guard duty. And what am I doing this fine Sunday? Guess. That's how youth and life are passing me by."

Ángel wants to go to "the zone", the place where people sign the guard log, so he can get himself on record and go home to bed. For now, he holds in the smoke from his drag and listens to Eduardo give vent to his frustration and disenchantment with everything. The cigar's ash, long and firm until now, drops to the ground under its own weight. Ángel draws a couple of times, but the cigar has gone out. He shakes it, removes the leftover ash with a fingernail, and lights it again.

"Didn't you leave Caibarién for Havana to get ahead? How am I supposed to save money as an 'analyst in film appreciation' so I can buy a house and start a family? Even if I got into dirty business and started riding the dollar, they'd still keep cutting off my power at night and giving me a morsel of bread every day, no butter, no milk."

Just then they hear the radio announcer's voice like a thunderclap through the Soviet receiver: "Fifty thousand watts of music power … K, double-A, Y … Little Rock."

"Turn it down a little," Ángel intervenes. "The lame woman from Vigilance could be listening through the blinds. Come on, let's move camp."

Father and son get up and sit on the step outside the store, away from where they could be overheard — far from the "ghost army of informing social climbers", as

Eduardo has just called them, before continuing with his diatribe:

"I'm sure she wouldn't think twice about dropping us in it if it helped her earn a few points and wangle a house in a better neighborhood, that despicable woman."

Ángel nods. The taste of the tobacco is growing more and more bitter and piercing as the cigar shrinks to its final quarter. Smoking is one of the few pleasures left to him in this life, he thinks, turning the butt around in his hand.

"Because that's what the system's done over the years: it's turned everyone against it. And everyone means you and me. We could become a source of suspicion for not clapping loudly enough, for skipping a meeting, or for making any kind of critical comment or joke."

The young man pauses abruptly and looks at his father for a few seconds.

"Let me have a couple puffs."

"No, it's bad for you. Leave that for the old guys. Besides, all that's left is a stub full of spit."

"I don't care. Everything I like is immoral, illegal or against revolutionary principles. Give it here a sec."

Ángel gives in. As soon as Eduardo takes his first drag, he removes the cigar from his mouth and gives it a couple of taps with his index finger.

"You shouldn't hit it constantly like a cigarette to shake off the ash. It'll fall off by itself. Only if it goes out: then you take it all off so you don't have trouble lighting it again.

*****

Eduardo takes another puff and passes the cigar to Ángel as he exhales. He's done complaining. He's ready for action. He has nothing to lose but his chains. Everything has to change as part of the universe's transformation. Impermanence. He enjoys how, in the stillness of the early morning, his mind easily fills with ideas and words of Marx,

Engels and even the Buddha. The truth is, he feels like a hero on the verge of plunging into a mythological adventure, one in which he'll abandon the known world as he confronts fabulous forces. He knows it won't be a feat he'll perform in order to return victorious and save his countrymen, but rather a one-way ticket to his own personal betterment. He has no problem with ascending to the skies only to make do with a modest fire in his hearth for the rest of his days. He'll be satisfied with slipping through the rocks of communism and yanking at least a hair from the fleece of the "brutal and turbulent North".

*****

"One thing's for sure: I have to get out of this country, but I don't want to leave you here alone," Eduardo blurts to his father in a whisper.

"Easy, my boy. No need to despair. Just to show you the true meaning of coincidence, do you remember Migue?"

"How could I forget him? If he hadn't loaned me money for your bail, you might still be locked up in 100 and Aldabó."

"Keep your voice down; these walls have ears. Well, it turns out that an acquaintance of his is selling a little fishing boat…"

Eduardo's eyes open wide as saucers when he hears the word "boat".

"And what does that have to do with us?"

"If you're so desperate…"

Ángel leaves the sentence unfinished and glances at what's left of the Reloba, which is threatening to go out again. He's not going to smoke anymore, but he's not going to crush it against the sidewalk, either. May it die the noble death it deserves, having granted him such pleasant company. He puts it out, tapping it several times with his middle finger, and lets it rest in the slot for water under the store's metal door. Now he's the one to look steadily at his son.

"Let's go home. I'll tell you there."

It's Official

> If the United States does not take swift and efficient measures to cease the incitement of illegal departures from Cuba, we will judge it our duty to instruct border troops not to impede any vessel that seeks to leave Cuba.
>
> (Fidel Castro Ruz, Cuban TV, August 5, 1994)

Time to Row

Evening falls on Saturday, August 13, 1994, and the island's northern coast seems to favorably receive anyone willing to take a chance. From Cayo Guajaba in the east, eleven people have just gone out to sea, including two minors. From Carbonera, ten; from Santa Cruz del Norte, six; and twelve from Bahía de Guadiana, toward the far west of the island.

In the Havana neighborhood of Santa Fe, which now shows no trace of the downpour that hit just half an hour ago, the tide rises again, returning to land those relatives and friends who, during their farewells at the second low tide, ventured as far as an islet a hundred yards offshore. One of the vessels is composed of four inner tubes around a sealed metal tank and a military truck tarp for a deck. Another is made of polystyrene with a wooden frame and platform. Among the floating artifacts of the so-called rafters are also a tractor roof mounted on irrigation pipes, and a spartan pair of inner tubes tied with bed sheets to a pallet.

Beneath the splendidly patterned clouds, pearled with the reddish light of the sun on the horizon, Ángel and Eduardo advance slowly along the sand toward the place where Castillo keeps his fishing boat. They've been supplying it with provisions to last them the several days their journey could take, as well as two machetes they'll use in case of unwelcome boardings. Ángel walks ahead, wearing light pants and a polyester pullover stamped with earth- and wine-colored motifs. Eduardo follows in Bermuda shorts, handmade sandals and a white long-sleeved shirt. They surreptitiously observe people of all ages climbing onto their naval improvisations and immediately getting to row, euphoric, as if they were starting a game. Some struggle to get onto a raft amid the hubbub and others try to prevent them from doing so. Some are applauded for their dexterity while others are booed for turning circles in the same spot. Some shout, others cry, and others just watch the show with curiosity. Jokes are hardly in short supply and neither is rum. A group of women on the narrow strip of sand can be heard singing:

Time to row, row, row
Time to row, row, row
Time to row, row, row
Virgin Mary'll be with you as you go

Twenty yards from Ángel and Eduardo, a figure in a straw hat and long sleeves sitting on an upturned bucket stands up, enters a zinc cabin and reappears next to a wooden keel.

*****

The greenish water first takes on a dark blue color, then goes bluish black as the boat, eight feet long and three feet wide, with a four-horsepower Johnson engine, enters the ocean and the night.

Eduardo is the first to replace Migue at the oars. He labors silently, unsure whether he's fleeing or has been expelled. Along with the Havana coast, he's leaving behind the web of limitations in which he had found himself utterly trapped at the age of thirty-two. His father seems bothered by the rolling movement; Migue, happy to have set out after six p.m. and thus avoid as much sun as possible.

"It's best to wait before starting the motor," remarks Migue as a raft with a motor and sail passes alongside them, a dozen people and a dog aboard. "The gas I've managed to come up with should last us more or less a quarter of the ride. For now, all we have to do is get away from the coast."

"I bet you guys don't know whose birthday it is," Ángel says after a brief silence.

"Whose?"

"El Fifo's. Don't you think this departure is a nice little present?"

"The best gift people could give him is to leave him all alone on his island," quips Eduardo.

*****

About six miles from Santa Fe, Migue announces that coastal navigation has come to an end and now they'll be making their way by the starts. Eduardo tries to abstract himself from Migue's labored explanations about the combined use of the time and the height of stars above the horizon but he suspects that he'll have a hard time putting up with his father's co-worker. Migue has struck him as pretty crazy ever since they met at the auto shop over ten years ago. And now, just what they need: he's also arrogant with it. But he knows his father wouldn't hop on a boat with just any weirdo, let alone bring his son along, too. He only hopes that, at forty-plus, Migue isn't the type of person who would set out on an undertaking like this without real knowledge and preparation. And that his bluster isn't a mask for ignorance.

*****

The water splashes into a sly foam against the shell of the boat, which advances on a course between east and northeast at a speed of two miles per hour.

"Down with Fidel! Down with communism!" four young men shout from a raft cobbled together from polystyrene, cloth-wrapped inner tubes, a railing and a tattered sail.

"See you in the Yuma!" Migue chimes in.

"There's no going back now, buddy," they reply.

Ángel raises a hand and shouts, "Good luck!"

His voice low, he praises Migue's caution in keeping the boat at a prudent distance from the raft. The little motor alone is enough of a temptation, he mutters in conclusion.

Eduardo, who can no longer make out any solid point along the horizon, believes they're no longer in the Caribbean, but rather in the Atlantic Ocean, that crucial channel of communication and global commerce he learned about in secondary school. The idea that all the oceans are connected beneath a tiny wooden boat, so tiny they can barely sit on their own asses inside it, suggests him the possibility that Migue might not have set them along a good course, which would be a mistake difficult to correct, maybe fatal. Panic needles into his brain like a parasite as he imagines the seabed. He can't assuage his unease as there is no way of knowing when or how this odyssey will end. To make matters worse, the afternoon heat is fading, and it won't be long before night falls and envelops everything. He rolls down his sleeves and buttons up his Chinese-style shirt. Then he rubs his hands together and blows on them. He wants to kick at the frame of the boat to ease the cold

151

he feels in his feet, exposed in their sandals. He needs to move, to get his blood circulating and keep his body heat up.

*****

Second dawn of the journey. The sea gleams and there's nothing in sight for miles around — except for a sky of silky, irregular white threads, harmoniously shared by both the moon and the sun.

"Let yourself rock along with the boat," Migue breaks the thick silence to address Ángel, who has vomited and looks at him despairingly.

Pulling a pack of Populares cigarettes and a lighter from the pocket of his work shirt, both tightly wrapped in a plastic bag, he adds, "Smoke while you still can, before I start the motor."

Eduardo's muscles hurt from the physical exertion and humidity, but he keeps rowing, fearful of erring at the current's mercy and being diverted toward Mexico or Europe.

*****

It's midday, clouds are scarce, and the boat maintains an east-by-northeast route at about three miles per hour. Ángel's arms and legs have gone stiff. He's been in the same uncomfortable position for far too long, and he doesn't know which is better, night or day. At night he can't see anything at all, so he feels disoriented and suspects all kinds of imminent danger, but during the day the sun burns him to a crisp. No one in their right mind would expose themselves to this punishing sun for more than half an hour. There's just nowhere to hide from it. He would have shed his synthetic pullover already had Migue not stopped him in his tracks.

*****

Migue has said they've got about forty out of the total ninety miles ahead of them before they reach Key West. According to the hasty assessment that Eduardo was able to do before they left, it's another ninety miles from there to the peninsula, and he hopes they won't have to row them.

"See Ursa Major over there?" Migue asks, in a new attempt to keep the conversation going.

While Ángel identifies the four brilliant stars along the base of the dipper and the three along the handle, Migue pulls out a plastic bottle of rum, takes a drink, makes a face, and shivers before explaining how, if they don't find Ursa Major, they can reach it through Virgo.

Eduardo pops a blister on his right hand with his teeth and sucks out the fluid. He says to himself that constellations are the product of human imagination: disjointed groups of stars, each of which follows its own course in the universe, quite distant from the others and bearing no relationship to them. Linking stars together, he forms an open-mouthed dragon between the Little Dipper and the big one, under which he recognizes an upside-down tie. Without straining to find it, he also suddenly notices, further down on the left, the shape of an enormous snake with a protruding belly and its head pointing toward the tie. He stops gazing upward. He has no desire to look out at the black, bottomless sea, either. Thanks to the sun or the night sky, they'll be able to get their bearings at times, but he knows they have no way of controlling the wind or the ocean currents — the forces that will really dictate their trajectory in extreme conditions.

A grayish strip rises up from the bottom of the sea, thrashes about and sinks back into the depths. Eduardo silently accepts the sign that the sea has no intention of taking pity on them. Then he hears his father beg for salvation from Our Lady of Charity, and notices that his lower jaw is trembling.

Migue hands the bottle to Ángel.

"Have a drink of rum to help you get rid of the chills and pass it to Eduardo. Did you see that? A whale shark. They're gentle creatures."

*****

The current accompanying Ángel's slow rowing brings them closer to Key West's southeastern coast early on the third morning of their journey. The wind blows in a favorable direction, the sea imitates it enthusiastically, and the boat, whose motor worked hitch-free for as long as the fuel lasted, now advances with almost equal fluidity, integrated into a harmonious synergy.

Eduardo has stretched out on the boat floor among bits of rope, cans of food and plastic containers filled with water and rum. Within just a couple of minutes, he falls into a deep sleep. Migue remains watchful, caressed by the wind and the low thud of the frame as it slices smoothly through the water. His comments about the Gulf Stream, "a river in the ocean", have triggered an uncomfortable feeling of insignificance in Ángel, overwhelmed as he is by the immensity of so much invisible sky and sea in the darkness. Continuing to row, he silently seeks out the lights of Cuba, knowing full well he won't find them. The island, along with fifty-four years of his life, have disappeared.

*****

The night gives way to a new morning and the boat moves with considerable momentum as it heads along its east-by-northeast course. Migue and Ángel have been taking turns at the oars. Ángel is resting when Migue signals to him with a jerk of his head: there is a pile of flotsam about fifty yards from them. It's the most ramshackle craft they've seen.

"Poor folks. Just think of how hard they must have worked to put that raft together and get all the way here," Ángel remarks.

"And the balls they needed to get onto it. An entire family could've lived for a whole year on the eight hundred bucks those inner tubes are worth in Havana," Migue adds.

Eight hundred dollars for both or just one? Ángel wonders before equating the price to that of a glass of water in a desert. "May Saint Barbara be with us, brother. At least this one's still sleeping," he says to his friend, crossing himself and gesturing toward Eduardo with his head.

*****

It smells like a storm is brewing up. Eduardo remembers the fascination he used to feel watching the regular undulations on the surface of waves in Santa María del Mar, Guanabo, La Playita de 16 and Monte Barreto. Who could have predicted then, when he'd stay captivated for entire minutes by the roundness, the emptiness and the sound of the waves as they broke against the shore, that one day he'd have to fight them for his life? How many men would you need on land to lift the boat bearing them on top and gliding along, unbridled, as if afraid that it might nosedive into the water? Six? Eight? You have to be on the high seas to understand how the waves play as easily with an ocean liner as with a dinghy. The energy found in this savage part of reality commands respect. It arouses fear.

*****

On the morning of the fourth day, the boat bounces, leaping up the sloping waves and falling back down amid the cold cascades that turn to foam on their skin and clothing. The waves, rising six and eight feet, seem to have no objective other than to surround them and noisily pound against them. There are moments when, after an agonizing pause, a biting, unexpected wave whips the boat. Sometimes they hear the roar of another approaching and have time to prepare themselves. A furious one lifts them up with a growl, another makes them lurch and a treacherous one nearly overturns them altogether. They struggle to survive amid hammer-blows of water and gusts of wind that ruthlessly lash against their heads and torsos, not knowing if they'll capsize, sink or be catapulted out. It's as if they'd been offered to the sea and it insisted on slowly wearing away the offering instead of digesting it all at once. Crawling around in the dark, they salvage what they can, use all their senses to get ahead of the waves and await them clinging to the boat.

The danger of falling into the sea suddenly becomes a reality when a wave catches Ángel off-guard, hitting him in the face as he momentarily relaxes his grip on the boat. He loses his balance, slips out of the boat, and falls headfirst into the sea. He stays underwater for a few seconds and the salt water finds its way into his stomach and lungs, threatening to strangle him. With his mouth at water level, he readies himself to call out, but the boat collides with his head.

Migue gives a shout about the thud against the hull. Eduardo tells him to hold onto his ankles and plunges halfway into the sea. Sharpening his senses, he searches blindly, touches clothing and tries to grab it, but it slips away from him. Then he pulls out his head, frantically gasping for air, and returns to his underwater search, feeling around with his hands. Still gripping Eduardo, Migue calls out his friend's name, then goes silent, listening intently. When Eduardo scrambles back into the boat, he calls out too. Frightened, he waits for his father's reply — but all he hears is the water beating against the wooden hull.

*****

A dead turtle is the only result yielded after more than twenty-four hours spent reading the sea's complex chemistry through constant explorations of its surface and depths. What does it need them for — those membranes that, like a reflecting screen, intensify the sensitivity of its eyes in dim light? What help is a strong sense of smell, a tool its species has been refining over hundreds of millions of years of evolution? It had detected blood but immediately lost the trail.

It senses a change in water pressure resulting from the activity around a boat. Within seconds, it positions itself strategically like a shadow beneath and behind the body making chaotic movements.

With an exploratory bite employing only a few dozen pounds of pressure, the teeth arranged inward in several rows leave less than eight inches of femur on one of the legs. Ángel notices some turbulence. He feels a yank at his body and a flash of heat in his right leg. He struggles to reposition himself so he can see where the jerking motion comes from, and can't see the stream of blood but feels a few strips of connecting tissue that hang down in tatters where his knee ought to be. A force much more violent than the previous one pushes him abruptly upward. Then he sees, a hand's length from his face, the beast's brownish skin that turns sickeningly white toward his own chest. He feels the jaws' pressure, the incisions of the tremendous serrated teeth and of the razor-sharp smaller ones. He yells as he strikes a blow to the blunt, scaly snout, between its expressionless eye and sinister smile, and water fills his lungs again to burn him from the inside. His attacker responds by shaking its sixteen-foot body and tearing apart what it's bitten off. Ángel remains face down, unmoving amid the buzzing and cracking sounds produced by what's left of his body.

*****

It returns to the depths, furious. A single bite informed it that the creature wasn't a seal or a sea lion — just a rafter with low body fat, like the surfer near Massachusetts, the diver in the warm, shallow waters of Panama City, and yesterday's rafter. Why are these scrawny, insipid figures the ones that keep crossing its path? This one even dared to counterattack. It should take a third bite, if only to practice the routine of letting the prey bleed to death and then going back for it. Otherwise, what will happen to its reputation as an invincible, murderous machine that doesn't even spare members of its own species? It will prove that, as a ruthless predator, aristocrat of the food chain, the tiger shark continues to occupy the highest echelon of the marine ecosystem.

Be Careful What You Wish for

The Yankees' double standard when it comes to immigration is manifested in the fact that they are admitting more rafters than individuals legally processed by the accord reached after Mariel ... The United States is not fulfilling its part of the 1984 agreement we negotiated with Reagan and which guaranteed 20 000 visas per year in exchange for our acceptance of some undesirables from Mariel. In accordance with that agreement, they should have granted 160 000 visas. However, they have only issued 11 000, while welcoming 13 200 illegal immigrants with open arms ... Once again, the Americans are launching a campaign to encourage illegality and civil disobedience. This has already led to several forcible entries into embassies, as well as armed hijackings of state vessels, one of which resulted in the death of a border officer ... Radio Martí has been announcing that a group of ships is coming to search for people along the Havana coast. It is hardly surprising that all the lumpenproletariat has gathered around the dock area ... For 35 years, the Yanks have been encouraging illegal departures from

Cuba even though they endanger the lives of people who do not want to leave the country. This kind of criminal, this kind of terrorist who hijacks boats and even kills, receives a hero's welcome in Miami … A group of antisocial elements has taken to the street in order to commit acts of vandalism … It is clear that these disturbances are being provoked by rumors of a US-funded sea bridge and that we cannot continue to serve as the custodians of the American coasts if the Yankees keep suffocating us economically and refusing to fulfill migration agreements. The Revolutionary Government cannot continue to protect the borders of the country that is provoking this situation. We must open our own so that everyone interested in leaving can do so unrestricted.

(Cuban press cables and dispatches from August 1994)

Emilia isn't fooled. She takes the Cuban press and all other media with a pinch of salt. She knows the crisis that's been brewing since July is the result of widespread social malaise and a much more complex situation. Seated once again before the marvel of the computer she uses on her weekend shift as an editorial assistant at *El Nuevo Herald*, she goes to the floppy disk unit and double-clicks on her own article for the Sunday supplement of another Miami paper, *El Cubanito*:

It is surprising how historical events are repeated. In April 1980, six people in a bus forcibly storm the Peruvian Embassy. A guard dies in the incident and the Peruvians opt for political asylum. The Cuban government withdraws protection from the diplomatic headquarters and some 11 000 people seek refuge there. Castro then opens Mariel port, through which over 125 000 leave the country. Ten years later, between July and August 1990, around 50 individuals make a surprise entrance into the Spanish, Czech, Belgian, Italian, Canadian and Swiss embassies, in what has come to be known as the "embassy crisis". This time, the island refuses to negotiate with the aspiring refugees, who must then return home. On September 9, 1993, eleven people burst into the Mexican Embassy. Following the negotiations prompted by the incident, because the other party is "a dear friend who has never turned its back on Cuba", Castro makes an exception to his migration policy and allows the occupiers to leave the country. Throughout May 1994, similar invasions occur in the Belgian and German embassies, as well as in the Chilean Consulate, and the island maintains its policy of non-negotiation with the occupiers, who number around 150.

The clock in the lower-right corner of the screen shows 22:50. Emilia sends her draft to the printer, gets to her feet, and wonders what Pepe will think of this third article when it appears in print. She acknowledges to herself that her ex-husband's opinion interests her as much as that of the newspaper's own readers, and that she draws much of her inspiration from their countless hours of conversation and life together.

She's got an hour of work left, tops. She'll make her last coffee of the night. Once at home, she'll do a hard-copy correction of this background section and develop the main idea: just a couple of months after the incidents at the European embassies and the Chilean Consulate, another Mariel is about to happen — a carbon copy. It's a theory, pure speculation, but it's how she sees and feels it. Her business is to discover truths between left- and right-wing discourses through her own experience, her observations, and her instinct.

Back in her revolving chair, she puts the printed copy face down between the keyboard and the monitor. Instead of collecting her things to leave, she follows the impulse to carry on typing:

> Cuba will first try the strategy it used in Camarioca in '65 with modest results, and again in Mariel in '80 with spectacular success. On both occasions, it set the course and pace of events, while its powerful neighbor remained on the defensive. The process is beyond familiar by now: there is instability and trouble on the island, Fidel tries to negotiate; the US refuses, he makes threats about the crisis; the Americans respond with mockery or their rhetoric of resistance, he opens the borders, first in secret, then publicly. And in the end it's the superpower that ends up overwhelmed and with no option other than to negotiate the new migration policy the little island needs.

"Be careful what you wish for", she imagines a headline reading in *Granma* or *Juventud Rebelde*. She doubts she can use anything similar in a Miami paper. Maybe "Carbon Copy", she muses, pursing her lips. She stands up again, walks all the way to the coffee maker this time, and notices that several reading lamps are still on in the editorial office in addition to the fluorescent lights — especially in the proofreading section and in Sports, where two souls hurry to amass their jargon before closing.

The Horse

Emilia enjoys the view offered by the Fort Lauderdale coast. She's been invited by a Catalan friend to spend the afternoon aboard a yacht owned by an Argentine rancher named Rogelio Romero. Studying the foredeck, she briefly imagines the letters "RR" branded on hundreds of cattle flanks and wonders what kind of boat could have been bought with the three thousand five hundred dollars she transferred to Spain. Her father and brother's journey will be infinitely more dangerous than her own in '80. The TV incessantly broadcasts images of desperate rafters, dehydrated, hypothermic, adrift.

This Rogelio fellow explains how he enjoys an unfettered life between the southern coasts of the peninsula and Lake Okeechobe. Every two months he makes a trip to Buenos Aires and his ranches in Patagonia, goes over the accounts with his administrators, and returns to the tropics. For him, there's nothing like the tropics, especially as southern Argentina has a cold climate for much of the year. He prefers heat and Hawaiian shirts, he says with a smile and a full mouth. The man is about forty and looks in great shape for his age. He's strapping, muscular and wealthy, and seems to exude testosterone. He's mentioned that he used to play rugby and Emilia can tell.

The conversation crackles like fireworks. Now the subject is the largest island in the Caribbean, with its enthralling beaches and landscapes, seized by the English, exchanged for the Florida peninsula, battleground of the Spanish-American War, almost another state in the US at a certain point in its history and a Soviet satellite in another, besides being an *agent provocateur* that brought the world to the brink of nuclear holocaust.

"And Castro won't die, the bastard," says Consol.

All eyes turn to Emilia. What do they want her to tell them? The attempts she can remember are the poison pen, the diving suit, the bazooka in the baseball stadium. She has heard about a chemical compound they'd planned to spread in his shoes so he'd lose his beard and, along with it, his power and charisma. But she'd prefer lighter chat about food or films, or even just about the community of neighbors in a marina like this one, in the world capital of yachting.

"I've always heard that, before the Revolution, Cuba was the third wealthiest nation in Latin America and a great agricultural country," says Rogelio. "How is it possible that people are starving there now? You see, my country's military was right on target when it carried out the coup in '76. If it weren't for them, and for the Uruguayan army and Pinochet in Chile, all of South America would have gone the way of Cuba."

The tanned Argentine Hercules has stamina — and it seems, from his intense blue-eyed gaze, he's attracted to her.

"That doesn't justify disappearances and torture, Rogelio," Consol intervenes.

"Don't forget that it was a dirty war, though. Sometimes wars involve certain excesses."

"Let's hope you've never had the chance to indulge in them," the Catalan woman retorts.

"I was never a soldier, Consol. But if I had been, I don't know how I would have acted."

"Let's not get sidetracked here," she says, trying to bring the conversation back on course. "I agree things can't be going so well on the island if the Cubans keep leaving any way they can. But there's the propaganda, too: it's the Cubans who get all the media attention even though the Coast Guard also intercepts as many or more Dominicans and Haitians. You'd have to ask the Mexicans why they emigrate despite the Free Trade Agreement. Thousands die on that other border every year. And I recently read that a quarter of all Argentines want to go live in the US or Europe."

As she utters this final sentence, she turns to Rogelio, who sits up straight and stuffs three olives into his mouth.

"Those are the lowlife Argentines, the ones who need to make a living elsewhere. Don't look at me, because that's not my situation. My money comes from Patagonia and I spend it here, not the other way around. You know I'm a rancher in a country that consumes and exports a lot of meat. You've come to some of my roasts."

Emilia pours herself some wine and surveys the remains of various tapas laid out on the white plastic table: pimento-stuffed olives, Brie and Gruyère, potato omelet, chorizo, sausage, coleslaw, and cucumber and carrot sticks. Her host, this paragon of South American criollo oligarchy, is an insufferable braggart, and she's disgusted by his attractiveness.

"I'll try to be clear," Consol continues. "What I mean is, communism and deprivation aside, there's a lot of media frenzy, and all sorts of rights for those who get themselves here and say, 'I claim the rights under the Cuban Adjustment Act'. I don't even want to imagine an Adjustment Act for Mexicans. Or the Chinese."

Rogelio opens his eyes as wide as saucers. Now he changes tack and directly addresses Emilia, who stares out at the sunset in silence.

"I was told you came through Mariel. On which boat?"

"On the *Lady Marion*."

"The *Lady Marion*? Seriously? With Bob the Brit?"

"I don't know if he was British or not, but he struck me as being very competent when it came to sailing. Weather conditions — and all kinds of conditions — weren't good at all."

"A really strange guy, obsessed with order and superstitious like you wouldn't believe. He says you shouldn't whistle 'cause it encourages the wind, and you should avoid stirring tea or coffee counterclockwise if you want to ward off storms. When he eats empanadas, he bites both ends first so the air can get inside. I don't know if he says this stuff as a joke, man."

"And you never will," says Consol, glancing toward the cabin and passing a spliff of hash to Emilia. "If you saw an Englishman on those stairs at this very moment, you wouldn't know if he was going down or coming up.

"You wanna go see the *Lady Marion* tomorrow?" the rancher asks Emilia, his eyes hypnotic. "Maybe it's docked at one of the municipal ports, which is where Bob is most of the time."

"Tomorrow I have an important commitment that might take all day," she says, after a drag, "but maybe some evening next week…"

"Are you sure? Because it's supposed to be a beautiful day. We could take a ride around the celebrities' islands and see the house where *Cocoon* was filmed, Julio Iglesias's place, Madonna's…"

"It's a shame, but I can't postpone what I have to do. Let me know if you want to go another day. If you have something to write on, I'll give you my number," she suggests.

"Just a second. I'll be right back."

While Rogelio disappears into the cabin, the joint once again comes around to Emilia, miraculously loosening the tension in her body. Consol's indistinct voices begin to reach her after a lag.

"Sorry," the rancher says, back again.

"I should tell you right now that I have no idea how I'll react when I see the *Lady Marion*," Emilia warns him.

"It's a free country. You can cry if you want, but I'd recommend that you smile and enjoy your freedom."

"I could also burst out laughing. Who knows?"

When she moves to drink from the glass he's filled for her, an uncomfortable rigidity seizes her arm. It feels so heavy that she's not sure she'll be able to reach the glass, and she's struggling to keep everything in focus. A gust of cold air brushes against her bare arms like a knife blade. Isn't it supposed to be a warm summer evening with clear skies?

Consol sits up and gestures that it's time to go. In the middle of a rushed goodbye, although Emilia can barely open her eyes, or perhaps for that very reason, the others agree that she should stay. She tries to organize her thoughts, to gather what she perceives around her into a coherent whole, to stand up without betraying her intoxicated state, but...

Luckily, Rogelio has taken hold of her and helps her descend the stairs from the deck to the cabin. She loses her balance again and he stays there to brace her — but this time he also caresses her shoulders, her hair, and her cheeks. She accepts the kiss he offers her, although she fears she'll be unable to return it with equal passion. Then she feels him fondling her breasts through her blouse and squeezing her buttocks. A large hand kneads her inner thighs.

She ends up in the bed, the rancher trying to unbutton her pants. At the same time, he thrusts his tongue into her mouth, bites her lips and twists his head to sniff at her. She feels too dizzy to consent and too dizzy to resist. Besides feeling desired, she'd like to be able to provide satisfaction with her body — older now, but still firm. She simplifies the task for the Argentine by tightening her belly, but immediately regrets it; having won the scuffle with the clasp, he nearly tears her bikini top so he can squeeze, pinch, lick and bite her breasts. His huge, greedy hand now slips under her bikini bottom. Possessed by anticipation, the male pants impatient, shakes his head and gropes as frenetically as a stud stamping the ground. Emilia avoids contact with his blazing eyes. She knows that it would take several men to hold him back, so she relaxes her hips and stops resisting. Her submission, however, only serves to unleash spasmodic thrusts that crush her against the bed, which repeatedly slams the wall of the boat. Emilia feels his intermittent jolts through her body, a convulsive climax and a snort. The man's head collapses clumsily onto her shoulder. Could he have had a heart attack?

Negative: he rolls away, deflated, spent, without deigning even to look at her.

Beyond the Ninety Miles

It is said that people shed an average of sixty liters of tears throughout their lives, but not a single one has slipped from Eduardo's eyes into the terrifying sea. Not because he's consciously blocked the thought of his loss, but because he needs to direct all his energy toward the present and can't let himself succumb to grief. He has accepted, in a moment of negligible brevity, that everything has a new order and that nothing can be salvaged of what used to be his life. Clinging to the oars, he scans his gaze across the infinite plain of waves and realizes they've spent hours thrashing around like a pair of possessed idiots. Since gods across latitudes and epochs have always had the bad habit of remaining impassive before human misfortune, as if nothing at all were happening down here, he asks Zeus directly why he insists on tormenting him. As he waits for an answer, he hears Migue's voice murmuring something about the Gulf Stream and glances down at the palms of his ruined hands, covered in blisters and slime. Maybe rowing is actually the best thing he can do to maintain his body heat, alleviate his aching muscles and keep his mind occupied.

*****

In the outdoor cafés, bars and restaurants at Mallory Dock, Key West, tourists and locals are enjoying the sunset, entertained by street musicians and artists. Four Cuban exiles wet their whistles with beer over a game of dominoes in Bahia Honda State Park. On Key Colony Beach, Crawl Key, some elderly British people chat unhurriedly as they play golf. In Islamorada, some Americans fish with lures, others scuba dive around the coral reef, and others shop, eat, or watch dolphins and sea lions as they frolic and pirouette.

Migue and Eduardo pass by from the east, parallel to the Overseas Highway 1, a sort of main artery for the whole island chain with its forty-two bridges. They can't see the coast. If they keep moving east by northeast, they won't even touch the peninsula.

Migue shifts his eyes from the stark bones of Eduardo's desolate face — he seems to have lost ten pounds since they left — to the raw sores that keep appearing on the young man's skin. He worries about whether he is becoming dangerously dehydrated, and doesn't discard the possibility of delirium or death.

*****

Eduardo studies the backs of the waves. If water is an amorphous substance, why does it manifest itself in endless, uniform spirals? A vertical skyward push fills the surface with curves that produce other curves, which multiply in turn to repeat the shape of the mother wave, like an echo. Gravity and the liquid's own tension must then push each little wave downward, and so on, he supposes. When he used to go to the beach, he always thought the water moved from horizon to shore. Now he sees it differently: what crosses the oceans is energy. The waves move out of their sheer need for renewal. What he observes around the boat is just a fractal image of infinity in perpetual motion. Only humans insist on viewing the world as an object. And, like the imbeciles they are, they keep on doing so as they grow up, age and are destroyed the same way they were created. Without grasping how dynamic, unstable and transitory the whole process is. Death had already tried to take him once at that sickening bar by the Havana port. It's taken his mother and now his father. If his time has come, he's ready. When a wave dies, it breaks amid a chaotic confusion of sound and foam, doesn't it? Well, he'll accept his fate with equal grace. He's prepared for the turning point. He just has to cast off the past, his heavy baggage — but what is left for fate to snatch away?

*****

As it had done every night, the dark sea produced an uncertainty and anguish stirring a desire to cry out in supplication. But the early morning is already under way and the only recourse is to await the dawn. The buzzing they hear — is it an engine crossing the sky? Could it be a light airplane operated by Brothers to the Rescue, the volunteer pilot organization that flies over the Straits of Florida in search of rafters, reporting their whereabouts to the American Coast Guard so they can launch a rescue mission? Unaware of the tourism services offered at such an hour by Key West and Marathon airports, Migue grabs the flashlight and makes intermittent signals skyward.

*****

Amid the tips, crests and shadows of the waves, Migue makes out a kind of spot, of indistinct shape, which could be a small raft. Noting that it isn't moving, he guides the boat in its direction, and warns Eduardo not to get close to anyone they might come across. This couldn't be farther from his companion's intentions. Eduardo hates the sight of the rafts, with or without passengers, and wouldn't wish the journey on his worst enemy.

About twenty yards away, Eduardo can see it's a body on an inner tube. The body of a man, skeletally thin, covered with ulcerations and in danger of slipping into the water through the hole. He can't tell whether the rafter is mulatto or albino, whether he's gone purple due to poor blood circulation or burns, or indeed whether what floats before them is a pile of mere bones.

Migue draws the boat closer and touches one of the legs with an oar. He touches it again, this time more firmly. The tube turns and moves away with the rigid figure still attached.

*****

In the mid-afternoon, a light but constant rain begins to fall, and Migue quenches his thirst with drops he collects in his upturned palms. He takes off his shirt and wrings it out over his open mouth. Eduardo follows his example and drinks as much as he can, feeling with relief how his skin satiates its own thirst through each precious drop. Migue recommends that he carefully use his shirt, moistened with fresh water, to rub his sores.

*****

Eduardo isn't at all sure that Migue's recent modification to their route is correct. He'll just have to believe him when he says they'll arrive in less than twelve hours. At least the boat is going in the same direction as the waves — a favorable, promising direction. But he wonders whether it's good or bad to feel hope. What was it doing in Pandora's box if it was something good? Why did it stay contained there if it wasn't? Meanwhile, Zeus doesn't mutter a word and, down here, the sun shines blindingly across the endless undulations of the ocean surface, which seems to boil. The water forms crests, foam, churning bubbles here and there, like countless boxers staring daggers at their opponents as they hop back and forth. Like lava. Like saws. There's not the merest trace of the biological diversity supposedly contained within it. It looks like lead or mercury. Eduardo feels like he's in a desert, with the same desperate thirst, the same feverish heat. The air scorches his lungs every time he inhales.

Suddenly, he thinks he can see an enormous suspension bridge covering the sea and obstructing his view of the horizon. He can't describe this vision to Migue, who will only think he's hallucinating. But that's exactly what he's seen: a bridge, the object that enables movement from one country to another, uniting territories and humans, and connecting lives.

*****

Migue touches Eduardo's forehead and neck. He has stopped trembling, but he's now in a deep, worrisome torpor. Migue estimates his temperature is at least forty degrees Celsius, maybe higher, and the only reason he isn't hallucinating is that he's just not strong enough. Then, he hears another aircraft approach.

It's a light Cessna plane, and it drops a small bundle that falls close to the boat before disappearing again. They've been spotted! He tries to keep calm as he takes up the oars and directs the boat toward the floating parcel. He can't believe that the adventure might actually be coming to a successful end.

When he sees that joy is also creeping into the ravaged face of his friend's son, his heart swells against his chest and he feels a knot in his throat. The two men lean forward painfully, embrace, let their heads rest on each other's shoulders and unreservedly burst into tears.

*****

The motorboat makes a half-circle around them. One of the young men aboard, with *U.S. Coast Guard* lettered in white across the orange background of his vest, slowly instructs them to put on the life jackets he's offering them. He speaks Spanish with a Mexican accent.

"Are you okay? Can you do it by yourself?" he asks Eduardo, noting that he doesn't appear to understand the instructions.

The man hasn't finished asking the second question when Eduardo collapses. Migue takes a step and leans forward to help, but, before he can do anything, a life jacket is pulled over his head almost by force.

"We're going to take him right away because he needs urgent attention. Another boat will come back for you. Okay?"

The two coast guards wrap Eduardo in a blanket and move him into the speedboat.

"Rest easy. All you have to do is wait here and not do anything else. Understood?"

Minutes later, the transfer of Migue from a speedboat to a military ship which has been out collecting rafters for days is not without complications: the latter is much taller and the former won't stop rocking.

During countless hours, people are brought on board the ship, their eyes almost out of their sockets, their faces and shoulders badly burnt, and their legs bitten by fish. Each is given water, a blanket, and a pair of flip-flops.

If Migue could see his reflection in the mirror, he'd notice that his own cheeks resemble crumpled brown paper. His straight hair is slick with dirt and sweat. His brown eyes, glassy and unsettled beneath his thick eyebrows, complete the portrait of distress that strikes pity into the heart of another rafter, a woman who has lost her 18-month-old daughter to the sea.

For Sale

The rafter arrivals have gone on for weeks and receive due attention in the American press. Bob follows the news with interest: more Cuban refugees reach Florida every day and, given the number of empty rafts, many are losing their lives in the straits. One day, Fox News announces that the Coast Guard has captured thirteen hundred, all of whom will be returned to their country. The next day, according to ABC News, they intercept over twenty-five hundred. CNN broadcasts images of a woman who starts to give birth on a raft.

As for the Cuban residents in the south of the peninsula, they seem to have gone crazy this summer. Some hoard provisions and basic necessities. Others pawn their houses to buy boats. Everywhere, the air is filled with a strange combination of hope and indignation. There are strikes, speeches, preparations and great euphoria. Why all the commotion? There won't be another Mariel, Bob feels like yelling.

Now that a potential buyer, who happens to be Cuban, is coming to see the *Lady Marion*, Bob remembers the three times he set sail from that same port in Key West, fourteen years ago, to bring islanders to the US. He'd done it with boyish enthusiasm and accompanied by hundreds of other boats. But if he were offered twice the money to set out on a similar journey today, close to retirement, he'd smile and calmly carry on with whatever he was doing — which, at present, is taking another sip from a refreshing pitcher of beer with lemonade.

He's begun the final stage of his plan to return to green and pleasant Albion, where he'll build his own Jerusalem. Next year he's heading off with his Dominican wife and their adorable brown-skinned, curly-haired son. He'll start packing up anytime now. His little house in South Miami has risen in value every year and it's now worth double what he paid for it in '80. It's in an attractive neighborhood, bordered by the University of Miami, Coral Gables and Pinecrest, with South Dixey Highway cutting across it diagonally. The area boasts restaurants, stores, a low crime rate and two hospitals that yield both jobs and tenants.

Guantánamo

Convinced that Castro will want to control the volume of irregular departures at will, the irate governor of Florida decides to declare an immigration emergency and demand the federal government's help in finding somewhere to locate the largest wave of Cuban refugees since '80. Although Washington is aware that the Cuban authorities are permitting small groups of people to leave without incident, they don't see another crisis approaching. The Attorney General insists that they're not considering any policy changes and dismisses the governor's reaction as disproportionate.

Unaware of these tensions between the southern state and the nation's capital, hundreds of rafters who have touched American soil approach Miami in a caravan of buses. Escorted by police vehicles and a helicopter, they smile and wave like sports stars at the residents who throw their hands in the air from the sidewalks, shouting phrases of welcome and support.

The neon lights and myriad of colors assault Eduardo's eyes. The few days he spent recovering in the temporary shelter for refugees on Stock Island suited him very well, but he can't wait to reach one of the hotels where, he has been told, they would be hosted until reunited with their families.

"And we spent a whole week like that, drifting, not getting anywhere much because we had to fend off the sharks with our oars. Those creatures were ten feet long and escorted us like the motorcycles you see over there," the man sitting next to him is saying.

Fortunately, Eduardo's silence is interrupted by the announcement of a ten-minute stop.

As soon as they're off the bus, residents approach them with cigarettes, candy and support. Seconds later, as Eduardo moves toward the counter of the cafeteria, where some of his travel companions pose for photos and offer quotes to the press, a strange silence takes hold of the place and all faces turn toward the wall-mounted TV.

Bill Clinton shifts his gaze between the cameras and the document he's reading aloud. Then, the anchor continues to report: following a meeting between the American president, the Florida governor and the president of the Cuban American National Foundation, Clinton has just announced that he will no longer allow the entry of Cubans seeking to emigrate to the US in an illegal, unofficial manner. All rafters intercepted at sea will be taken to the

Guantanamo Bay Naval Base, where they will remain indefinitely until relocated to third countries. Only those who have reached American soil before the announcement will be granted asylum in accordance with the Cuban Adjustment Act of 1966.

Krome - Miami Beach

Some two hundred new arrivals throng the lobby, gardens and hallways of Miami's Civic Center Inn. They haven't caused any trouble yet and seem very grateful for the break. Their presence unnerves a couple of employees, but the hotel management hasn't received any complaints and the Department of Justice is paying the bill.

"This is the life!" shouts one from the edge of the pool, a can of Old Milwaukee in his hand.

"The sweet life!" agrees another with a big, hairy belly, floating face-up.

Eduardo's spirits have risen, infected by those of his compatriots. He is stunned by the level of luxury at the hotel: hot showers, air conditioning, color TV channels. The refugee resettlement staff have given him a bag of toiletries, all impossible to find in Cuba, and today he's taken three showers so far, in addition to brushing his teeth before and after breakfast and lunch. He can't believe the turn his life has taken. He can't remember ever having felt this way before. And the day should have more in store: he's been told that in the evening he'll be taken to a place called Krome, in the southwest of Miami-Dade County, which has capacity for several hundred refugees. Anticipating the avalanche of Cubans, the migrants from other Latin American countries and China have been transported to Louisiana and Texas. Anything but Guantanamo, he thinks: he's sure that conditions in this

Krome place will be a lot better than in a Cuban "school-goes-to-the-countryside" barrack, and that he won't go without water, soap, toothpaste, food or electricity.

*****

Hundreds of south Florida residents have risen early and come to the old missile base in the Everglades. It had been abandoned for some time but was remodeled in 1980 to process Marielitos. Emilia remembers its transformation and is amazed by the fact that, fourteen years later, the plot of land and buildings are still being used more or less for the same purpose. Pressed against the wire fence, she waits for an immigration officer to come out and read the list of detainees. It's the second time she's come since she called Cuba and one of Ángel's neighbors said that her father and brother had disappeared from the neighborhood.

She's feeling nauseous but has no intention of subjecting herself to a medical check-up now, let alone pressing charges against the stupid cowboy. She has enough problems as it is. She hates him. Why did he have to be so brutish? Of course there will be a way to get rid of this pregnancy, she thinks, trying to calm herself. She's not giving birth to a rapist's child. For now, she's requested the week off so she can think carefully about what to do and come to Krome as many times as necessary.

She and Pepe always had clear goals and priorities: first, they had to grow as people and "progress". They wouldn't start a family until they had the necessary financial stability. At one point, they achieved enough of a financial cushion that they could relax a bit and help relatives in Cuba, but priorities and goals kept postponing motherhood. Which is why she finds it so ironic that life has played such a spectacular trick on her now. She never wanted to be a sparrow that could be satisfied by any old breadcrumb, making its nest and hatching chicks in any old place. Nor did she ever suspect that she'd end up the hen that no one had seen in her, including herself. But here she is, clucking about, collecting her two dear chicks — never again will she abandon them. With another on the way.

She has felt marginalized so many times for not having reproduced. If a woman doesn't want to have children, people practically write her off. Now, thanks to another of fate's great ironies, she can put an end to this kind of discrimination in her own case. She lives a much more settled life than before, with more means and more control. At Miami Dade College, she is assigned the number of class hours she wishes to teach; a few months ago, she passed the trial period as an editorial assistant at *El Nuevo Herald*; she still writes for *El Cubanito*; and those endless days in the medical clinic have been left far, far behind. Sometimes it takes drastic changes to create enough push for advancement, she muses. When she quit her job at the clinic, she achieved the unthinkable: she was given work to do at home; only transcriptions, paid on a job-by-job basis. She recognizes that her wild years are behind her, and that the happy-go-lucky *criollita* isn't coming back. But Emilia Ribot Hernández still has a lot to give. And motherhood, giving life to a tiny being and looking after it with the greatest zeal and excitement, could very well become her greatest adventure, the most beautiful journey she's ever going to take. It's an enormous responsibility, spending entire nights attentive to its breathing, and then protecting it, feeding it, educating it. But even just — just? — being pregnant, she feels that the elusive meaning of happiness has been revealed to her: a pure, unconditional love; faultless and forever.

*****

Emilia can't believe what she's hearing.

"Cuba, yes! Castro, no!" shouts the crowd around her.

Where is the connection between these phrases and the place they're calling them out from? She wants to make them understand that Fidel isn't in the detention center himself, but she fears they'll lynch her right then and there if she tries. Meanwhile, the shouting intensifies and she reminds herself that many of the visitors have been waiting in line since the night before. She understands that the wait, their frustration and the scorching heat all aggravate their mood — and is not surprised that the crowd is now raising shouts of protest at the Immigration and Naturalization Service agents, and singing the Cuban national anthem.

The situation reminds Emilia of incidents back in 1980, particularly the riot at Fort Chaffee. The Marielitos' presence at that other base had agitated the residents of Barling, a small nearby town which, with the influx of Cubans, had become the eleventh most populated city in Arkansas. The refugees and their irregular behavior had led their terrified neighbors to arm themselves to the teeth. They had also provoked a visit from the Ku Klux Klan, which inevitably produced more trouble. But Emilia is convinced that, more than anything else, it was the desperation and frustration in response to their seemingly interminable confinement that led some to declare a hunger strike, almost three hundred to escape and wander the streets of Barling, and then twenty thousand to riot and set the barracks on fire. When President Clinton, then the governor of Arkansas, mobilized the National Guard, the melee resulted in about fifty wounded on both sides. And two dead Cubans.

*****

On the other side of the fence along Krome Avenue, convinced of the inherent superiority of all things foreign after a lifetime of scarcity and hardship on the island, the refugees are delighted to take a shower, put on their orange uniforms — higher quality and better made than clothing in Cuba — and eat decent food.

Eduardo tries to answer an Immigration and Naturalization agent's questions as coherently as possible.

"Do you have relatives in the United States?"

"Have you ever been incarcerated?"

"Have you been in the military in Cuba?"

"Have you worked for the government there?"

"Do you have any kind of infectious disease?"

"Is it true that everyone on the island has a raft or is building one?"

Eduardo is distracted by the sound of women's voices singing the Cuban national anthem. He thinks he knows the place quite well by now, and over in that direction is a men's dormitory. Where could the singing be coming from, then?

The interview ends abruptly, sooner than he'd expected. He doesn't feel at all satisfied but the other steps seem to go well: the results from the tuberculosis and syphilis tests he was given on arrival have come back negative, and he now has his I-385 card stamped by the Public Health Service, which means he can "integrate himself into the community". The only problem is, since he lost his sister's contact information during the journey, he's one of many without close family members here to receive them. He's still a detainee, he thinks, wearily picking up a newspaper from a chair in the common area and taking it with him to the toilet.

It remains to be seen whether this decision to send them to Guantanamo will prevent more Cubans from attempting the trip. And if they keep coming, we don't know what will happen when Guantanamo and Krome are full. Those are some of the questions that have yet to be answered.

Eduardo intently reads this remark by a member of the Senate Intelligence Committee. The friends he's made in the center have told him that the same Democratic senator had spoken with them personally and assured them that they wouldn't be sent back to Cuba. And so this man, with the positions he holds, has no answers? Of course, he won't breathe a word of what he's just read to his fellow detainees; he doesn't want to be written off as the prophet of doom. Fortunately, the promises of assistance aren't coming from politicians alone. Charitable agencies are doing everything possible to find them homes and work, whether inside the state or elsewhere. He harbors a hope of setting out at any moment for Kentucky, Texas, Oregon, Connecticut or another state through the program run by the Catholic Agency and the Department of Immigration. Last night some activists had come to explain it.

"Eduardo!"

Who the hell needs him so urgently that they'd come looking for him here?

"Eduardo Ribot!"

"Here. What is it?"

"Are you Eduardo Ribot?"

"Yes. What's going on?"

"Man, someone out there's been looking for you for a while."

*****

The brilliance streaming through the window prevents Eduardo from recognizing his sister until she's practically right in front of him. He approaches her almost floating, in a state of grace, needing neither gestures nor words to express his joy.

"And Papi? Where's Papi? Didn't he come with you?" Emilia asks, looking around nervously.

"In Cuba. Easy now. I'll tell you later."

Hugging his sister, Eduardo feels strong, wise and at peace. More the protector than the protected.

*****

There's a traffic jam outside the detention center — the authorities have decided to block all access to the complex. To drown out her own thoughts and make the wait more bearable, Emilia switches on the radio in her '83 Honda Accord, metallic blue with a film of dirt in which someone has written "Also available in blue".

According to the announcer, the Americans have reinforced their patrolling of the Cuban coasts with thirty planes and eight thousand soldiers. With the goal of preventing islanders from reaching the US, the navy and the Coast Guard have diverted more than sixty ships normally used to patrol fisheries and against drug trafficking.

The vehicle gradually leaves the traffic jam and, to the sound of one of the latest musical hits, Emilia tells her brother about how she's been renting a studio in a Miami Beach condo since her divorce from Pepe. It's small, but it has all the comforts of modern living and fantastic views. As they leave signs and billboards behind, the conversation turns to landlords, rents, mortgages, insurance and personal loans.

Unable to fix the hinge of his sister's glasses, Eduardo seems to be concentrating on the landscape gliding past the window. Is he following what she is saying to him? Emilia moves on from the clunky money-oriented chitchat to a diatribe against Miami Cubans, backstitched with warnings about specific people. She finds her brother a bit too pleased with himself at having attained his little piece of heaven. This makes him all the more vulnerable.

*****

From the navy blue futon, Emilia follows her brother with her eyes. He hasn't stopped pacing the small studio. In Havana, he would often wander around lost in his own thoughts but relaxed. Now he seems much more reserved and rigid; he breathes intensely, and drinks and smokes like a man possessed.

"Do I look different to you in some way?"

Silence.

"I know I haven't sent you any photos for a while..."

Eduardo studies her face and her hair.

"I'm pregnant!"

"No way! Congratulations, sis! But you said that you and Pepe..."

"No, Pepe's not the father. Don't ask me who it is. It doesn't matter whether he's an American or a Bulgarian, but it's not Pepe. I'm the mother, father and holy spirit."

"Amen! Incredible news! I'll celebrate with another lager."

Emilia watches how her brother half closes his eyes. There is restlessness in his expression and his forehead is sprinkled with drops of sweat. His confident and graceful manners have been replaced with an agitation that is beginning to provoke in her a state of nervous tension, which certainly isn't good for the baby.

"And have you thought about possible names?" he asks, facing the open refrigerator.

"Please! You'll see that there's no time to even go to the toilet around here."

*****

Second afternoon at Emilia's. Eduardo opens another can of Coors and pauses in front of the small altar dedicated to Saint Lazarus, by the wall dividing the tiny kitchen from the rest of the studio. He notices that, besides crutches, rags and dogs, the old leper has a six-inch Montecristo cigar at his feet, as well as a little glass containing what looks like red wine. Then he walks to the studio's only window. He doesn't need a balcony to be entranced by the late-afternoon sun reflecting on the white façades and terracotta roofs. The blanket of clouds he had noticed the last time he looked out has completely disappeared, and he's soothed by the colors of the lawns, plants and flowers. Could he be starting to collect himself after the traumatic crossing of the straits? The price has been high, very high, but he's so convinced of the infinite opportunities awaiting him that he can only take a deep breath and appreciate the harmony around him. He knows he has his sister's help, too.

He steps away from the window, takes another cigarette from the box Emilia has left on the countertop, but doesn't light it. Instead, he walks from one end of the room to the other with the cigarette in his mouth. The time has come to talk about the journey. He looks at the futon where his sister is seated, takes a step toward her, pauses and moves forward again, this time more purposefully. He ends up sitting down beside Emilia.

While he rubs his knees with the palms of his hands, a mournful shadow crosses his face. He begins to murmur, barely opening his mouth, and suddenly the words tumble out. His lips tremble as they separate, press together and are distorted in an expression of pain.

Blood

Eduardo is home alone, itching to smoke. He's just heated the last drop of coffee left in the thermos and brings it into the living room, stopping again in front of Saint Lazarus to admire the Montecristo Especial No. 2 cigar amongst the offerings. With the saint's permission, he takes the cigar and slowly studies the sheen of the smooth outer leaf enveloping a deftly twisted body with no bumps. He's never smoked anything so elegant. His father probably hadn't, either. He presses on it, massaging it in a circular fashion. It's firm, compact, but not too stiff. He brings it to his ear, still rolling it between his fingers. As he walks to the window, he wonders if cigars, like rum, get better over time.

When he catches a glimpse of his own face in the mirror on the wall, he's accosted by a hotchpotch of disconnected images. He lifts the cigar to his mouth and looks for his split self in the cheekbones, eyes and hair in the reflection. When will they stop, the duplication and multiplication that subject him to this sensory overload? Lacking an answer — whether his own or one from his mirror-self — he turns back to old Lazarus. Eduardo feels on his own skin the pain of the tatters brushing against the saint's wounds. He asks him for forgiveness and takes a pair of scissors from a clay jar on the shelf beside the altar.

It occurs to him that the object between his teeth could catapult him into enlightenment, to some higher consciousness that will return everything to its rightful place. He removes it from his mouth and makes a cut about one eighth of an inch from the end, but the wrapper threatens to detach. Has he ruined the head with his inexpert cut? Nothing that can't be solved. He refixes the cap with saliva and takes a trial drag through the newly formed opening. The suction isn't bad. A little tight perhaps, but it's been a long time since he's enjoyed a cigar, let alone one like this. Even before lighting it, he's already detected an exquisite aroma of wood. He takes the cigar from his mouth to give it another look. His desire to smoke is growing monstrous. Imbued by the imminence of a well-cured leaf's dense smoke, he stands with his back to the open window and strikes a match. Its flame arcs toward the cigar while he turns it and sucks, as he's seen the old smokers do. As he saw his father do.

Just the smell and taste he'd imagined, he thinks, relaxing instantly, his mouth full of smoke. From the way the lit end looks, the combustion seems perfect. The suction feels tight but maybe that's because of its caliber — just over half an inch — or his own lack of technique, or both. He's going to smoke it with a slow cadence, not forcing it, adapting himself to it, and what it wants to give him.

Walking around the studio, he appreciates the kindness offered to him by the first third of the cigar. He holds the smoke in his mouth for another instant and then blows it out. The smell evokes a memory of the cocoa toasted in his Cerro neighborhood, and of freight handlers using the empty sacks to cover their heads and backs, like hooded monks. Without a doubt, this Montecristo was designed to be smoked alone, he thinks. Not only has it evaporated all his worries, but it has also transported him back to his childhood in Havana and brought him back to Miami in seconds.

Then, his thoughts turn to some of the Cuban immigrants he's met. Some are painters and poets; some stay at home with their small children because it's more expensive to go out and work just to pay for childcare; some work part-time in politics; some are unemployed; some are depressed. Others are Santeria leaders, witch doctors or Palo priests. As he listens to Simon and Garfunkel singing an old Peruvian song from the adjacent studio, his new trade comes to him in an epiphany. Reader and interpreter of cigars!

"Hand of Orula, Yoruba parody. Tell me ... No, I can't hear you. Ecue-Yamba, Ecue-Yamba. Orisha ob-la-di. Sensemayá la-da. *Eccola qua*, Artemis of Ephesus. Greetings. Here goes my litany of Palo Mayombe and Banquo *du bard anglais*. Smoke? Smoke, you say?"

Along these lines he supposes he could start his reading and interpretation of a good Cohiba. He won't have to dress in white, or wear a *guayabera* shirt, or a scarf or straw hat on his head. None of that nonsense. A good rum that won't distort the reading is all he'll need for his paranormal faculties to flourish, for the spirits to converse.

"Sambia, first among all things," he says, and begins to rotate the cigar in his hand.

After asking the name and birthday of the interested party, and warming things up with Scotch whiskey if the American embargo insists on depriving him of seven-year Havana Club rum, he'd proceed to read a Cohiba Lancero. He'll have to learn how to do it without forcing his breath so much, to smoke a little more elegantly, but the important thing is inspiration and everything else is gibberish.

"See those little black dots around the crown? You listen to everything I'm going to say, but remember it's not set in stone because this is an initial reading and the signs aren't clearly defined yet. I usually start with the worst and I can tell you that I see pretty ugly things in most people: all kinds of separations, jealousy, gossip, entanglements, betrayals... In your case, you just have to be careful with money, which seems to be your Achilles heel. Now take a look at these little white flakes. That's a new love, which will bring new friendships along with it. See that red dot over here? That could mean an oversight concerning your health, but you're not stupid and you'll take care of yourself. It could also be a fleeting excitement, a disappointment, but we all have some of those, don't we? There's no need for me to keep showing you the concrete manifestations on the cigar of what I'm going to tell you today because, as I'm sure you understand, I can't just go around divulging sacred secrets. But let's get to the point. I don't see any betrayals or hidden enemies. Envy, yes, and ingratitude, but you won't let them throw you off course."

Facing the effigy of the saint once more, he removes the little glass of wine from its gloomy surrounds, shakes a finger to shoo away the swarm of fruit flies along the edge, sniffs, and takes a sip. He'd be flooded with clients from faraway places like Las Vegas, New York or Madrid.

"*Pour votre esprit*, Sarabanda," he says, now standing before a three-legged iron cauldron in a corner, sprayed with rum from his mouth. "Let it out! Let it out! *Oui, oui. Ochún, Obatalá, merci bien.* Here we are, giving it our all. *Olofi, chenche. Olofi, yényere*, I can see you want to talk. A drink? Ready to receive you. Pray tell me about this person I have in front of me."

His mind stays blank for an instant before returning to the Cohiba, which, besides containing an intense note of leather, has created half an inch of compact, light gray ash, with black and white discs and streaks. Ash: a world in which to decipher the future in love, professional life, family and health. And smoke: infinite possibilities. Even the matchstick and the tree that gave it life!

"Eleguá, Changó, Yemayá, hear the plea of this woman who has come all the way from Quebec. Her soul seeks consolation and her future is written in the skies, to which you and only you have the key. Open the doors of her destiny," he recites after lifting his chin, looking up at the ceiling and expelling a mouthful of smoke that fills the room.

He lets the ash drop onto a white plate and contemplates it steadily, as if a light trance had overcome him.

"You'll suffer a little more, dear friend, but your sorrow will leave you, little by little," he tells the young woman sitting cross-legged on a Tunisian rug. "You will receive a deep and gradual happiness that will lighten your body and soul. I see that you'll meet a new love and this time you'll learn to keep it. Now return home and have faith in Yemayá. We'll have a follow-up session, of course, but six months from now. Come back in half a year, not before, unless you feel a pressing need to consult me on some other matter. I think we can stop this session here; I have another one in less than half an hour and I need to be disconnected from everything before then. You can't imagine how draining this work is. As we discussed, that'll be two hundred."

Eduardo takes the four bills printed with the image of Ulysses S. Grant that the Canadian holds out to him and deposits them on the oak desk, under the altar candle holder. Invoking Yemayá, he passes his hands through the flame and places them on the girl, who weeps a few tears.

He helps her to her feet.

"Go, good woman, and may joy and energy grow within you."

With ardent eyes, the woman moves away, walking backward so she doesn't turn her back to him, as she has been instructed. Her gaze wanders to the clairvoyant's scar, but she immediately returns it to the floor and continues her backward exit.

Once the woman has crossed the threshold, Eduardo inserts the four bills into the wad of the same denomination. Who would have guessed that, when he crossed a foul-smelling street and a young woman appeared before him with a greasy hand, asking for a handkerchief, all that would lead to all this? He remembers taking her in with his eyes and his desire as he invented fantasies that remained huddled in some corner of his memory. Now his memory revives and suggests this new act of colossal buffoonery — which will earn him money just as that prior one earned him a glass of malt, an empanada and the love of a beautiful girl.

*****

Five years later, stretched out in a bathrobe on the veranda adjacent to the pool in a Key Biscayne condo, where he has bought a three-bedroom apartment with an ocean view, Eduardo watches his nephew's movements. He enjoys staying with him for a couple of hours at a time so Emilia can catch up on her work. The child awakens a tenderness in him that he's never experienced before.

The boy stops playing on the patch of lawn beside the veranda and approaches the pool. He wants his uncle to get into the water with him. Eduardo shakes his head and becomes more alert. Fortunately, Emilia has finished her work and is now here with them. The cute Brazilian neighbor has arrived, too, leading her daughter by the hand; the girl is just a few months older than Angelito. Within seconds, the children start playing their games on the grass — under the watchful eyes of their mothers, who say the beach is more fun than the pool.

Eduardo doesn't yet feel hot enough for a swim. He'll wait a little longer, savoring his mojito, before taking a dip. He thinks about how, if he hadn't let Beatriz go, if the two of them hadn't condemned to oblivion the little one growing in her belly, maybe he wouldn't feel so alone now. But it's also possible that such a situation wouldn't have gotten him out of Cuba and, instead, would have aged the student whose palm he read that rainy afternoon, exhausting her with the routines still imposed by the system on the island. Now the little one would be going around, neck wrapped in a red scarf, shouting empty slogans and wracked with hunger. Of course he wouldn't be so alone now, he thinks again, drinking the rest of his mojito through the ice cubes and placing the glass on the floor, beside the Sunday edition of *El Nuevo Herald*.

"And I would've had a little grandson, or granddaughter," Ángel interrupts.

Eyes half closed, Eduardo sees his father approaching, accompanied by the smell of salt residue and the noisy crashing of choppy waves. He moves at a good clip and with a resigned elegance despite lacking both legs. Skeins of veins, tendons and nerves hang from his two short stumps, and his abdomen is torn open, exposing his intestines. But the expression on his face is exactly as it always was.

"Don't you see that you already have a grandson?" Eduardo responds, shaking off his initial confusion. "Emilia gave him to you. He's beautiful and has the same name as you."

Ángel nods and flashes his peculiar smile — as if he weren't sunk deep in the Caribbean, processed by the digestive system of a damned shark. Why does he smile so lovingly?

"It looks like the shark was merciless with you."

As he makes this remark, Eduardo struggles to hold back the tears that threaten to spill — unlike the ones he couldn't release when his father disappeared into the dark sea.

"Everyone has the right to eat," Ángel says, still smiling, and now reclining in the deck chair beside Eduardo.

"I can't tell you how happy I am that you've come to see us. I've wanted to talk with you so badly. You left without giving me time to tell you all sorts of things."

"Don't worry. It's almost always like that. Life's events don't usually leave much time for people to open their hearts. We only do it after a departure. That's why those of us who leave usually come back, at least for a little while, to continue unfinished conversations. So now we can talk about whatever you want. But it's not like we have to be all serious or melodramatic, either."

"Have you seen that Emilia writes for *El Nuevo Herald*?" Eduardo asks, seeing that his father has picked up the newspaper from underneath the chair. "She's a top-notch journalist."

"I can see that. She always did have her own opinions," Ángel observes, his eyes scanning the article, which is indeed signed by Emilia Ribot.

"Her opinion pieces are some of the clearest that are published here. The other day she showed that, statistically, there are more Haitian and Dominican rafters than Cubans if we take into account that…"

"'Faced with the wet-foot, dry-foot policy allowing only those who make it to the shore to stay, Cubans suddenly changed their battered rafts for the speedboats of human traffickers'," Ángel reads aloud. "Evolution leap aside, this is another remarkable article, like the one about the emigration pressure cooker that El Fifo manipulates at whim. She's certainly got talent and inspiration. I'm so happy for her."

Father and son continue discussing politics as if nothing had happened that far-off early morning on the high seas; as if they'd seen each other just a few hours ago, and yesterday, and the day before yesterday.

"If she stays this objective, I wouldn't be surprised if they censor her one of these days. Hey, you wouldn't have one of those Cohibas for me, would you?"

"Just a second," Eduardo answers before dashing into the apartment.

Rummaging in the drawers of the oak desk where he stores the tools of his trade, he touches the old scrap of paper, which he pulls out and re-reads:

Dear son,
I hope you can forgive me for what I'm going to do in your absence. One day you'll understand that I'm doing it for the good of our family. If you get out on leave and see this note, go to the Peruvian Embassy, which is where I'm going now with Mireya and Sofia. First try to get in touch with your sister. I haven't been able to speak with her because I don't have the address of the beach house where she is now, and Mireya doesn't want to wait any longer.
Sending you a big hug and hoping to see you soon,
Dad

He remembers finding it on the table in their Cerro tenement room one of the times he went AWOL from military service. And hiding it in his French edition of *The*

Golden Bough, because it was too late to seek asylum: the embassy had already been cordoned off.

On his next visit to the room, however, his father was there as if nothing had happened. Neither of them ever mentioned the goodbye note.

When he returns to the pool with the cigar, Ángel isn't in the deck chair, or the water, or anywhere to be seen.

"In the end, I didn't go because I couldn't stand the idea of being far away from you and Emilia. What a shame she and Pepe got divorced. They were a good couple for a while," Ángel admits, back in the deck chair, reaching out a hand for the cigar his son has brought him. "At least she looks happy now with that beautiful kid."

"He's going to be a real heartthrob, isn't he?"

"Yeah, and I don't give a damn who the father is: he's my grandson, and that's that. You take care of him as if he were your own son. And your sister, too, who loves you like crazy."

"You can see that I spoil her like a queen. She says the dinner I made her on Sunday was a total revelation: *insalata caprese* in the shape of an Italian flag and *linguine alla puttanesca*. Today I'm going to surprise her with a 'Cuban night': rice and beans, yucca with mojo sauce, fried plantains, and a roll of pork loin with chorizo and pepper-stuffed olives inside. It's enough to make you lick your fingers, huh?"

"She needs to be spoiled," insists Ángel.

"And what do you think I'm doing? I take them out at least twice a week. Next month, we're going on a trip to San Francisco, because we're basically done with Orlando and we just got back from New York and Boston. We have nothing to complain about, Papi. Believe me, we're really happy. I can't tell you how much I wish you'd made it."

"Who says I didn't make it? I made it. And so did your mom. In you two, our blood. Get it into your head: we all made it."

Eduardo sits up, but his father is no longer in the deck chair, although the smoke from his cigar keeps floating through the air. Or is it coming from Eduardo's? He takes a few steps toward the veranda railing, looks around in all directions but can't see him anywhere. And so he lifts his eyes over the sea, to where Havana must be.

"In you two, our blood," he repeats aloud, his gaze lost along the horizon of waves.

THE END

Interaction with the Author

Thank you for reading *Waves*. If you have enjoyed the book and would consider recommending it, perhaps you could devote a few minutes of your time to writing a review on the website of the ebook distributor you purchased it from. Other readers with similar interests would appreciate your thoughts.

If you would like to share any honest, constructive comments, please write to **info@joseramontorres.com**.

My second novel is a journey in the opposite direction to that of *Waves*, from the First World to the Third World. You will find an excerpt on **www.joseramontorres.com**.

To stay in touch through social media, you can use Facebook (**www.facebook.com/jrtorresaguila**) and Twitter (**twitter.com/JRTorresWriter**).

Thank you again,

José Ramón Torres
Cambridge, United Kingdom
September 30, 2015

www.ingramcontent.com/pod-product-compliance
Lightning Source LLC
Chambersburg PA
CBHW070947120726
47910CB00004B/1150